Mia yawned, stretched and sat back on the sofa. "Sweet dreams, little Drew."

Hank waited until she lolled against the cushions, her hand close to the baby's side, before heading into the kitchen. When he returned five minutes later with two coffees, she was asleep.

Well, well. She looked so tired, he couldn't disturb her. He got rid of the mugs, then retrieved a comforter and extra blanket from his bed. He spread the comforter over the floor. With great care he moved the slumbering Drew and his blanket onto it.

Next he removed Mia's boots. She sighed and stretched out on the sofa. Hank draped the extra blanket over her and paused to touch her face. The skin was as soft as he'd imagined, as soft as the baby's. The faint scent of baby powder and woman tickled his senses.

Feelings he didn't understand clogged his throat and he swallowed thickly. He knew he should drop his hand, stand up and head the hell outside. Yet he couldn't seem to move....

Dear Reader,

No matter who we are, we all carry emotional baggage. Whether our burdens are huge weights or small loads, whether we fight to free ourselves or hide away depends on the individual and the circumstances. I wrote Mia and Hank's story to explore how two people, each with their own private demons, come to trust each other and fall in love through the perfect catalyst—an innocent baby.

Thanks to a heavy burden of misplaced guilt, Mia has chosen to hide from life. I set this story in a remote, woodsy town in Washington State to highlight her isolation. Hank has chosen to work through his guilt by creating a monument to a lost friend in the same rural town, where he, too, can hide awhile. However, as the only neighbors within miles, they are forced to rely on each other again and again. And when Drew comes along... But I'm not about to ruin the story by telling you what happens.

I hope you care about Mia, Hank and Drew as much as I do. Please e-mail or write and let me know.

Happy reading!

Sincerely,

Ann Roth

P.S I love to hear from readers. Write me c/o P.O. Box 25003, Seattle WA 98165-1903 or e-mail me at ATROTH@comcast.net. Please visit my Web site at www.annroth.net, where you'll get the latest news as well as a delicious recipe of the month. And don't forget the contest. Enter to win a free book!

The
Baby Inheritance
Ann Roth

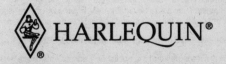

TORONTO • NEW YORK • LONDON
AMSTERDAM • PARIS • SYDNEY • HAMBURG
STOCKHOLM • ATHENS • TOKYO • MILAN • MADRID
PRAGUE • WARSAW • BUDAPEST • AUCKLAND

ISBN 0-373-75107-9

THE BABY INHERITANCE

To my editor, Allison Lyons.
I appreciate your support more than you'll ever know.

Don't miss any of our special offers. Write to us at the
following address for information on our newest releases.

Harlequin Reader Service
U.S.: 3010 Walden Ave., P.O. Box 1325, Buffalo, NY 14269
Canadian: P.O. Box 609, Fort Erie, Ont. L2A 5X3

Chapter One

The bright halogen beam that sliced through the chill night air hit Hank Adams square in the eyes. Momentarily blinded, he jerked to a stop, averted his gaze and shut off his smaller, less powerful flashlight.

Even without sight, he knew who wielded that harsh light. Mia Barker. The two of them had banged heads more than a few times over the past couple of weeks. She didn't much like him, and he didn't much care.

Liar.

"What in the world are you doing on this side of the madrona trees so late at night?" she asked in her deceptively soft voice.

Hank imagined her large eyes narrowed in warning: get off my property.

Her three-legged mutt, Ginger, limp-trotted over, nudging her snout at his thigh. The dog seemed to think he was okay, so he ignored Mia's unspoken order to leave.

"Hello, girl." He shoved his flashlight into the pocket of his denim jacket, then hunkered down to scratch behind the dog's ears. "I'm looking for Nugget," he told Mia. "He got out before dark and hasn't come back. I thought he might be here with you."

The beam of light dropped from Hank's face to the ground. While his eyes readjusted, he lumbered to a standing position. Though it had been nearly two years since the accident, he hadn't regained all his strength and stamina, and tonight every muscle ached. Too many hours stomping over plowed-up earth, scaling ladders and hefting building supplies. He needed a massage, but there were no massage therapists in Forest Glen, Washington. Even if there had been, he'd never subject anyone to seeing, let alone touching, the ugly scars on his torso.

"Nugget hasn't been here today." Mia shot a glance over her shoulder, toward the large hawk's pen, recently vacated by an injured wild bird she'd nursed back to health. Nugget liked to sniff around the perimeter, then go into his inbred pointer routine. "You shouldn't have let him run off, not around here," she said with obvious disapproval. "It's not safe."

Feeling like a scolded boy, Hank set his jaw. As

if he didn't know that. Forest Glen's rural location in the Olympic foothills meant animals of all kinds freely roamed the area. Over the years coyotes, the occasional wolf and even a cougar had been spotted—or so he'd heard. In the two weeks since he'd parked his trailer here, he had yet to see anything besides the usual birds, squirrels and raccoons.

"I didn't figure Nugget would learn how to open the trailer door," he said.

With the light now trained at the ground, Hank saw Mia clearly. She wore a shapeless, light-colored flannel nightie that reached her calves, and clutched a large, woolen shawl around her shoulders. The unlaced boots on her feet looked as if she'd toed into them in a hurry.

She was his neighbor, the only neighbor within a ten-mile radius. He wondered if he'd awakened her, or if, like him, she had difficulty sleeping.

"It's close to midnight, and you were up and pounding on that house of yours at dawn. Don't you ever rest?" she asked as if reading his thoughts.

After putting in a twelve-hour-plus day he longed to fall into bed and let sleep claim him. But he shook his head. "Not until I find my dog."

In the beat that followed his statement the silent woods around them grew quieter yet. Even the gurgling creek running along the perimeter of both properties seemed subdued. Ginger issued an uneasy, whining sound, and worry sluiced through Hank.

"Ginger and I'll keep an eye out for Nugget," Mia said, this time in a kinder tone. "I hope you find him." She paused, tucking her hair behind her ears. "If he needs medical attention, you bring him straight over. Anytime, day or night."

"Thanks, Doc."

Hank appreciated the offer, but hoped he wouldn't need his neighbor's veterinary services. He wasn't here to make friends or to rely on anyone other than the temporary crew he'd hired. He wanted only to build the house, win the award, put the place up for sale and leave.

"Well then, good night," Mia said.

She aimed the flashlight like a rifle at a point between two madronas, showing him where she expected him to go—back onto his own property.

Sliding his flashlight from his pocket, he turned in the opposite direction, heading rapidly toward the stream and woods beyond and gritting his teeth against his protesting muscles. Her stronger light followed and shot out ahead of him, illuminating the way across a ground jumbled with wet spring grass, twigs, half-imbedded rocks and occasional mole holes.

He stumbled on a tree root concealed in the

shadows, swearing under his breath and wincing, but not slowing his pace. Damn woman made him self-conscious. When the arc of her light no longer touched him or the land, he heaved a relieved breath.

Then, compelled for some reason he couldn't name, he halted and pivoted toward Mia's place. Her flashlight now off, he could barely make out her form as she moved silently toward her cabin. She pulled open the door, emitting a thick slab of rose-hued light as warm and inviting as a blazing fire.

Hank couldn't help comparing her cozy cabin to the utilitarian trailer that doubled as his office and house. House, not home. Even Nugget knew the difference. Lately he'd spent more time at Mia's than with Hank.

A one-eared, flat-nosed tomcat, the ugliest cat Hank had ever seen, appeared on the threshold as if welcoming Mia and Ginger home.

The two animals touched noses before the dog pushed past and disappeared inside. Mia scooped up the feline, cuddling it against her chest. Like a voyeur, Hank drank in the homey scene, wondering how a creature like that sounded when it purred. For nestled in the heat from Mia's body, cushioned against her soft breasts, he was surely purring. Hank swallowed against a pang of longing.

But warm and welcoming as Mia's place was, she lived as solitary a life as Hank did. Her land and cabin were on the outer edge of town. True, she ran her vet clinic from here, but in sparsely populated Forest Glen, patients didn't exactly line up to see her. There was a part-time assistant, Sookie Patterson, Hank knew, because her husband, Bart, worked for him. The rest of the time, it seemed Mia was alone.

Hank speculated on that, wondering what personal demons drove her to stay separate. She didn't seem to mind the solitude; actually, she seemed content. Which made her unlike any woman he knew.

Mia and the tomcat slipped inside. The door closed, shutting out the light and warmth. Hank chafed his arms, but his thin jacket and the damp air hadn't caused his chill. That came from the lonely ache inside his chest. An ache he'd carried so long, it had become an old friend.

He whistled softly, calling for his dog as he resumed his search.

THE FOLLOWING MORNING, just as the paws on Mia's funky cat clock hit eight-thirty and the tea water started to boil, Ginger woofed at the kitchen door. Rags swished his ratty kitty tail and glanced nervously from the door to Ginger to Mia, and back to the door.

Since the front door was reserved for strangers, company and patients, it must be a friend. "You like people," she reminded Rags in a soothing voice.

The latch lifted and Sookie Patterson came in. The small, slim woman was Mia's veterinary assistant and her closest friend.

"Hey, you," Mia said with a smile as she pulled two blue earthenware mugs from the old maple cabinet. "You're a half hour early this morning."

"I know."

Sookie wiped her feet on the mat and gave Ginger and Rags each a warm hello pat. Satisfied with the greeting, the animals curled up together on the doggie mattress near the heat vent.

"We haven't had a chance to schmooze for a while, and I figured this was a good morning for it." Her cheeks red with cold, she shut the door firmly behind her. The odor of clean, fresh air clung to her.

"I'd love that," Mia said.

Sookie hung her plaid wool jacket on the crowded coatrack beside the door, then rubbed her arms. "I could use something hot to drink."

"Sit and I'll make tea." Mia packed two tea balls with peppermint tea leaves and placed one in each mug. The fragrant smell of mint permeated the kitchen as she poured water from the steaming kettle.

"Can you believe how chilly it is this morning?" Sookie's short, curly brown hair bounced as she sat in her customary place near the window. "There's frost on the ground, and it's the third week of April!"

"I hope this cold doesn't last, and I hope it hasn't killed my flowers." Mindful of spilling, Mia carried the mugs to the oak table in the corner. Like the sixty-year-old cabin, it was scarred, but comfortable and sturdy.

"As long as your new neighbor keeps Bart employed, I can live with ruined flowers," Sookie said.

Mia had spent a restless night fretting over Hank and his lost dog. Actually not just last night. The man had unsettled her since the day he'd parked his fancy oversize trailer on the cleared part of what had been old Doc Murphy's five-acre homestead. She was tired of Hank's intrusion into what had been a quiet, orderly existence, and didn't want to think or to talk about him anymore. Lips compressed, she sank onto her chair.

"Hank's a little brusque, but he's not that bad," Sookie said as if reading her thoughts. "Right now, aside from Bart, he's my favorite man in the world."

She liked Hank, but then, so did just about everybody in town. So what if he'd razed Doc's old cabin and plowed up a good chunk of the meadow it had stood on? Doc had only been dead a few months and his property on the market all of three weeks.

Rumor was that Hank had paid cash for the property. Then he'd lost no time spreading the word about the modern house-beautiful he intended to build over the next five months. Thanks to Hank, Bart and five others had good jobs and steady pay-checks. In the economically depressed town of 2,450, that was a very good thing.

Even so, Mia resented the noise and upheaval.

"He's good-looking, too," Sookie added. "In a brooding sort of way."

Mia concentrated on removing the tea ball and placing it on a small plate. "I suppose."

Hank Adams was tall, lean and muscular, with piercing whiskey-brown eyes and a generous mouth some women might find sexy—if he ever bothered to smile. With or without a smile, the man did not appeal to Mia, not in any way.

"I get the feeling you don't like Hank." Sookie shot her a curious frown. "What's the deal?"

Mia didn't even need to think about that. She had a list of complaints, which she rattled off, using her fingers to count. "For starters, the mess. And the lack of privacy. Hank may own five acres, but he's building the house just two hundred fifty feet away."

She nodded at the large window behind Sookie, then at the smaller one over the kitchen sink, beyond which a row of trees heavy with yellow-green leaves and fat, pink buds somewhat obstructed her view of Hank's project. Thank goodness for small favors. But aside from scattered trees and bushes, the front of her cabin and clinic were visible from the construction site.

"With him or his men coming and going at all hours, I don't dare leave the curtains open at night. Last, I don't like the noise. It disturbs the animals. Can't you hear it?"

She cocked her head and listened. So did Sookie. A thin, erratic droning sound carried through the trees, the buzz of some machine at work. Mia wrinkled her nose. "I want my world peaceful and quiet, the way it was." She sighed. "Why didn't Hank choose someplace closer to Seattle to build his house? That's where his company is based."

"Bart says he aims to win some big architecture award with the house, and the rural setting is important to the overall design." Sookie leaned toward her, her blue eyes bright with excitement. "Just think what will happen if he wins. Everyone will want to settle here." She rubbed her hands together in expectation. "We'll have an economic boom for sure."

"Oh, joy," Mia deadpanned. "Do we really want a bunch of builders tearing up our woods?"

"If it means permanent jobs around here, definitely." Though there was no one else in the room, Sookie leaned even closer and lowered her voice. "They say Hank Adams is a man with a past."

"Hmm," Mia said. She sipped her tea. Any fool with eyes could see Hank was hurting from something. She was used to reading animals, who couldn't talk, and she read Hank the same way. His gruff manner didn't fool her. Underneath the hard exterior was a lonely man yearning for solace.

The nurturing part of her wanted to reach out and give him the comfort he sought, while her logical side recoiled. Mia sided with logic—people were unpredictable. She preferred to spend her time and efforts on animals, who were loyal and loving.

"A man of mystery," Sookie continued. "How romantic."

"Not to me."

Her friend gave her a sideways look. "He's your neighbor, your only neighbor. Aren't you even curious about him?"

"No," Mia snapped.

Sookie's jaw dropped. Mia, too, was surprised by her sharp tone, and hurried to soften it.

"We all have our shadows, and his are none of my business." She directed a pointed frown at her friend. "Or yours." Sookie opened her mouth, but Mia cut her off. "Our hawk actually ate this morning," she commented, neatly changing the subject.

Two days earlier the clinic had taken charge of the wounded red-tailed male, a young adult coming into his prime. He'd been hit by a vehicle, possibly one of the trucks coming and going next door.

With Sookie's help, Mia had cleaned his infected

wing and bloodied chest and injected antibiotics. If all went according to plan, as the bird healed and gained strength, Mia would transfer him from his small cage in the clinic's recovery room to the large flight pen outside. By late summer he'd be ready to return to the wild.

"I sure hope he makes it," Mia said.

"With your gifted touch he stands a good chance. You're as good if not better than having his own mama tending over him."

Mia knew she was a capable veterinarian. She also knew she'd make a rotten mother. She scoffed. "I'm nobody's mama, Sookie."

"Well, you'd be a darn fine one. First things first, though. We need to find you a man."

Mia rolled her eyes. Not that again.

Sookie, who'd found true love at the age of thirty, believed every female should find her mate and settle down to wedded bliss. But some women—Mia included—just weren't made for love, marriage and happily-ever-after. Every person she'd ever loved had either died or left, and she wouldn't put herself through that kind of emotional pain ever again.

"Sookie, Sookie." She offered her friend a smile. "How many times do I have to tell you, I don't mind being alone. My life is full. I'm doing okay."

So she wasn't exactly happy. So sometimes, especially late at night, an empty feeling stole over her, as if she were missing out on something. At least she had her peace of mind.

"Really," she added in an effort to convince herself.

Sookie eyed her with concern. "Are you okay?"

"I didn't sleep well last night." Mia shrugged. "Hank stopped by around midnight, looking for his dog," she explained, giving up her resolution not to talk about the man.

"Nugget, missing? Goodness, I hope Hank found him."

"So do I. Between the cold snap and the wild animals prowling around out there, I shudder to think what could happen."

With Sookie's help, Mia had stitched up a fair number of wounded animals and euthanized some that had been too far gone.

"When you dropped off Bart this morning, did you happen to see Nugget?" Mia asked hopefully.

"No, but then, I wasn't exactly looking." Mia's friend flushed. "Since Bart got that job, he can't keep his hands off me," she confided with a grin. "Amazing what a regular paycheck will do for a man's libido."

"Ooh." Mia grinned back, pleased for her friend.

And envious. Sookie and Bart had married nearly two years ago. They were crazy in love and still as wild for each other as honeymooners.

Not that Mia wanted what they had. She especially didn't want marriage. Because a husband likely would want babies… She frowned into her half-empty cup. A premonition she couldn't identify niggled through her. Though the room was a comfortable seventy degrees, suddenly she felt cold.

Oblivious, Sookie fiddled with the napkin holder, two ceramic cocker spaniels attached to a wooden base—a grateful patient's gift last Christmas. "I'm going over to the site on my noon break, so Bart and I can eat lunch together. I'll ask Hank about Nugget then, unless—"

The front doorbell buzzed, putting an end to the conversation. "Who can that be?" Mia glanced at her watch. "It's a quarter to nine. Everybody knows we don't open for another fifteen minutes."

"Probably Marnie Beeler." Sookie rose. "I scheduled Peachie first thing for her annual shots, and you know how Marnie is about that dog."

Mia knew the older woman well. A widow, she doted on her Pomeranian, treating him like a grandchild. "Always early," she sighed as she, too, stood. "Tell her I'll be with her shortly." She scooped up both mugs and carried them to the sink.

"Right. Thanks for the tea." Sookie was halfway through the cozy kitchen when the doorbell buzzed again. "I'm coming, I'm coming," she muttered as she hurried toward the living room and front door.

Mia ducked into the small utility room off the

kitchen where she kept her lab coats. She slipped one on, then patted her chin-length hair into place. Now she was ready for Peachie and whatever else the day brought.

When the phone rang, she shot a pleased grin at Ginger and Rags. "Looks like it's going to be a busy day."

The dog yawned and the cat opened one eye, then burrowed closer to the canine's side and promptly went back to sleep. They didn't care at all, but Mia did. She liked busy days.

Stepping around the animals, she picked up the phone. "Mia Barker."

"Good morning, Ms. Barker," said a brisk female voice. "Please hold for Judith Ellison, attorney-at-law."

"Who?" Mia asked, but the tinny music let her know she'd been placed on hold.

She didn't know a Judith Ellison, did she? Frowning, she searched her mind, coming up blank. The only attorneys she knew were the two who lived in town. They were both men, didn't have their secretaries make their calls, and unless their pets needed attention, they had no business with her.

Maybe someone was suing her. But who, and why? She could think of no reason. As the seconds ticked by, unease shivered through her, much like her earlier premonition. Mia trusted her feelings, relied on her instincts. Working with animals, she had to.

Right now, those instincts warned her she was about to get some unexpected news—bad news. Bracing herself, she pulled the phone cord taut and sank onto a kitchen chair.

Chapter Two

Sensing her growing agitation, Ginger and Rags hovered anxiously around Mia's feet as Judith Ellison, an attorney in Bellingham, Washington, introduced herself over the phone.

Pleasantries over, she cleared her throat. "I'm afraid I've got bad news," she said, her corporate voice appropriately softened. "Your cousin, Rosanne Mathis, has died."

"Oh, no." Mia hooked her feet around the chair legs and buried her face in one hand.

Their mothers, both long dead, had been sisters. Rosanne was Mia's only living relative—or had been. She lived two hundred miles away, in Bellingham, and they kept in touch through Christmas cards and occasional phone calls.

They were the same age, twenty-nine. Too young to die. Tears filled Mia's eyes, overflowed and rolled down her cheeks. "I talked to her just three weeks ago, after her son was born."

Dear God, the baby. She gripped the receiver. "What about Drew?"

"He's fine."

"Thank heavens. What happened?"

"Apparently the baby was at the sitter's," the attorney explained. "Your cousin was on her way to pick him up. A drunk driver hit her. She died instantly."

"Then she didn't suffer. That's something, I guess." Sorrow clogged Mia's throat as old memories bubbled up. Rosanne had been the only person besides Mia who knew the truth—that Mia hadn't seen her mother since moving into this very cabin with Gran twenty-four years ago, a month after her father had taken off and seven months after Gracie's death. Mother was searching for peace of mind, Gran had explained. Apparently she never found it, for Mia had never seen or spoken with her again.

Now Rosanne, too, was gone.

"Funeral services are scheduled for the day after tomorrow," Judith Ellison said.

Mia had appointments but would cancel them. She jotted down the particulars. "Thank you."

"There's more," the attorney said. "As you may or may not know, Andrew's father has relinquished any and all paternal rights. Ms. Mathis has named you legal guardian."

Certain she'd misunderstood, Mia gave her head a rapid shake. "What was that?"

"Once you meet with a social worker and complete the paperwork, you'll be able to adopt the boy."

Unable to speak, Mia gasped. After what had happened with Gracie? Was her cousin nuts? Sensing her distress, Ginger whined and Rags jumped onto her lap. Mia stared dumbly at the cat.

"Ms. Barker?"

Rags butted her knuckle. She curled her shaking fingers in his thick fur. "I—I loved my cousin, but choosing me to raise Drew is a horrible mistake," she stammered.

"According to the will I have in front of me, you are Andrew Mathis's legal guardian. Right now he's in foster care, waiting for you. How soon can you pick him up?"

GRUNTING WITH EFFORT at Mia's front door, Hank re-settled his whimpering dog against his chest. At seventy-five pounds, Nugget was no lightweight. Hank wasn't sure he could maintain his hold on the red setter. Murmuring words of comfort to the dog, he leaned his aching hip against the cold plank walls, easing his burden.

Nearby, the drone of a skill saw mingled with men's voices. His men. From Hank's vantage point he couldn't see them, but the work noises reassured him. He hadn't wanted to leave the site, but the nasty gash in Nugget's paw had forced his hand. The dog had stuck by his side through the worst of times. Now it was Hank's turn to do the same.

"Answer the door," he muttered between gritted teeth as he glanced at the gutter, the old wooden kind you rarely saw anymore. It appeared to be clogged. He'd mention that to Mia—if she ever answered the door.

He scowled at the Closed sign propped in the window. She'd said to come by anytime, day or night. Well dammit, he'd rung the buzzer twice already, no easy feat for a man hanging on to a dog with both hands. Where the hell was she? Fresh out of patience, he hefted his burden higher and eased away from the wall. As he reached his elbow toward the buzzer yet again, the latch clicked. Nugget's ears raised hopefully.

"About time," Hank muttered.

The door swung open. Sookie stood there, short, bouncy and openmouthed as if surprised. "You're not Marnie."

"Who?"

"Marnie Beeler, our nine o'clock. She's always early." Her eyes were wide as she stepped back. "Mia said you were out looking for Nugget last night." She shut the door. "Looks like you found him. Come on in."

While Sookie turned the window sign to Open and tugged the drapes apart, Hank stepped inside Mia's for the first time, into an inviting space that looked more like a living room than a waiting room. A colorful, braided rug added warmth to worn but gleaming hardwood floors. The knotty pine walls, overstuffed sofa and comfortable-looking armchairs beckoned him to sit and stay awhile.

A wishful pang caught him in the gut, and for a moment he wanted to do just that. Since Mia didn't much like him, she'd have a fit if he stayed. His sudden snicker earned a sharp look from Sookie before her concerned gaze moved to the bloody rag wrapped around Nugget's paw.

"What happened to your foot, sweetie?"

At that moment Ginger limped into the room, the nails on her three paws tattooing an odd rhythm as she trotted toward Nugget. The ugly cat followed, his flimsy tail high and his head proud, as if he thought himself the handsomest of cats. At the sight of the animals, Nugget yowled mournfully. Hating that his dog was suffering, Hank grimaced.

"Fool dog didn't come home until dawn." He shook his head, both relieved and worried. "He must have cut himself during the night. I tried to take care of the injury myself, but the wound's too deep."

"He'll need antibiotics and possibly stitches,"

Sookie said as she headed toward a door off the side of the room. "Follow me."

She opened the door and held it for Hank. They headed down a hallway lit by a pair of skylights. He'd noticed this newer part of the cabin from outside. The original building must be at least sixty years old, but this section had been added within the last five years. Unlike the country warmth he'd just left, the clinic was spare and modern, all business except for the humorous black-and-white photos of animals along the cream-colored plaster walls. Feeling more comfortable here, he released a breath.

They passed several closed doors before Sookie led them into a small room. "Why don't you put Nugget on the exam table?" she said, gesturing toward the gleaming stainless steel surface.

As Hank complied, a dog down the hall barked in loud, staccato yips.

"Yoo-hoo," an elderly female voice called.

"That sounds like Marnie," Sookie said. "Try to keep Nugget still until Mia gets here, okay? I think she's on the phone." Offering a quick reassuring smile, she slipped through the door, closing it softly behind her.

In the ensuing silence, muffled sounds of voices and animals filtered into the room. Nugget's eyes widened in panic.

"Easy, big guy." Hank patted the quivering dog and

continued to murmur reassurances as he scanned the room. A small, stainless steel sink and white Mylar cabinets lined one wall. The rest of the place was painted a soothing blue and contained framed, detailed anatomical sketches of dogs and cats. Mia's diplomas hung on one wall. A typical vet's exam room.

He squinted at the diplomas. She'd graduated with honors from both undergraduate and veterinary school. With those credentials, she could have opened a practice in any big city. Why choose Podunk, U.S.A.?

He heard footsteps, then voices in the room next door—Mia's and an older, unfamiliar female voice that must belong to Marnie Whoever-She-Was. Within moments, Mia knocked, then opened the door. Her face, normally glowing with health, was drawn and ashen. Shell-shocked.

In the two weeks he'd known her, Hank had never seen her in such a state. A sensation he couldn't immediately identify squeezed his chest. Concern, he realized with dismay. An emotion he no longer allowed himself except in relation to work. He shook off the feeling. Unless Mia's troubles prevented her from taking care of his dog, they were none of his business.

Yet he couldn't stop his question, telling himself he needed to know for Nugget's sake. "You okay?" he asked gruffly.

"Fine," she said with a brisk nod and a tight smile.

She squared her shoulders and in a blink shoved aside whatever was bothering her. That impressed the hell out of him.

Eyes on Nugget's bloodied paw, she gently unwrapped the rags. "What happened to you?" she asked in a low, crooning tone.

The dog stopped whining, angled his head and gazed at her with adoration. Though Hank had never seen her work, his dog's reaction reassured him. If Nugget trusted her, then he guessed he would, too.

"Beats me," he replied. "He crawled home like this a few hours ago."

Mia's mouth tightened and he knew she was silently censuring him—the same as she had out loud last evening—for letting his dog escape and run loose. He braced for the verbal lashing he figured he deserved.

Thankfully she spared him that. She washed and dried her hands, all the while talking in a soothing voice designed to calm the dog.

"Let's take a look at that paw. Sookie's next door," she told Hank. "Would you mind giving me a hand? Stay close to Nugget and hold on to him."

Glad for something to do, Hank kept a grasp on the setter's nape while Mia injected Novocain near the injury. As they waited for the shot to take effect, she gathered supplies from various cabinets.

She examined the paw in concentrated silence, then glanced at Hank. "It's a deep gash, but I think stitches will take care of the problem." She patted the dog's back. "You're a lucky fella. Ginger lost a leg from her night in the woods."

So Mia's concern for Nugget last night had been based on experience. "What happened?" Hank asked.

"She stepped into an illegal trap someone had set," Mia explained, cleaning the wound as she spoke.

He imagined that happening to Nugget and cringed. "I hope you caught the bast—jerk who set that trap."

She shook her head. "Unfortunately, no. After I amputated Ginger's leg, the couple she belonged to decided to give her up."

"So you took her."

"Someone had to. The paw should be numb now."

She pulled the jagged edges of skin together, then stitched them shut. As she worked, Hank kept his gaze on her small, competent hands. Under her skillful ministrations, his pain dulled by the painkiller, Nugget didn't seem to mind.

With the animal relaxed, Hank's thoughts shifted from dog to woman. What would those healing hands feel like on his damaged flesh?

A bitter smirk tugged his mouth. Useless question, since no woman would ever again see or touch his body. Not after Kristin. One look at his hideous scars and she'd run so fast, he'd barely had time to blink. It had been nearly two years but it hurt as if it were yesterday. And he wasn't about to waste time thinking about *that*. With the stubborn determination he used to tame his physical needs, he pushed away the mental pain.

Mia tied off the thread and straightened. "All done."

As she was disposing of the used supplies, Sookie entered the room.

"I weighed Peachie. She's ready for her shots." Seeing Nugget, she patted the dog's head. "I told Marnie you'd be a while longer."

"Thanks." Mia wrapped a clean bandage around Nugget's paw. "It would be a good idea if the bandage stayed on overnight." She administered a penicillin shot. "He'll need antibiotics three times a day for five days. Can he take pills, or would you prefer liquid?"

"Pills are fine."

She nodded, then washed up. She and Sookie consulted in low voices, then the assistant left to retrieve the medication.

"I'd like to check on Nugget's progress in four days," Mia said. As soon as the words were out, she stopped short, then bit her lip, looking as if she'd just received a rude reminder. "Actually, I'll be up in Bellingham then." Leaning heavily against the counter, she rubbed her temples with the tips of her fingers. "Better make that six days." She counted on her fingers. "Next Thursday."

"You're the doc."

Something or someone had her plenty upset. Hank wanted to know who and what, but managed to curtail his curiosity, instead asking a different question. "Headache?"

"You wouldn't believe how bad."

She closed her eyes and continued the self-massage. Her hair had sprung loose from behind her ears, the light brown color contrasting sharply with her smooth, too pale face. Was her skin as soft as it looked? Hank gripped the exam table to stop himself from running the pad of his thumb across her cheek to find out.

Mia's eyes opened. Ears burning, he yanked his attention to Nugget.

To his relief, she didn't seem to notice his discomfort. "So I'll see you on Thursday," she repeated, pushing away from the counter.

"You keep biting your lip that way and you'll need stitches like you gave my dog."

She unclamped her teeth from her lower lip and tried a smile. It didn't extend beyond the tentative curl of her lips, and quickly faded.

Her shoulders hunched and she pulled her elbows close to her sides, all turned into herself. If she got any paler, he feared she'd faint.

"You look like you need to sit down."

"I'm all right," she said, but when he cupped her slender shoulders and guided her into the small room's lone chair, an orange vinyl thing, she didn't fight him.

Her head barely reached his shoulders and her bones felt small and delicate. Which astonished him, because she carried herself with such pride and strength he'd figured she was bigger and more solid.

"You want to talk about it?" he asked, surprising himself.

So much for minding his own business.

She sighed heavily. "Let's just say, a few minutes before you and Nugget showed up, my life turned upside down." She glanced at the door, again gnawing at her poor chewed lip. "I wonder where Sookie went. It can't take this long to find those pills."

Ignoring her change of subject, Hank asked, "What turned your life upside down?"

Laughing without humor, she shook her head. "You wouldn't believe it if I told you."

"Try me," he urged, then clamped his mouth shut. *Jeez, buddy, put a zipper on it.*

She looked up at him, silent for several moments. Just as Hank decided she wasn't going to talk, she gave a small shrug.

"Everyone will know soon enough, so why not? I just found out that my cousin died yesterday." Swallowing, she stared at her lap, tracing the black creases of her slacks with her finger. "She was only twenty-nine. Killed instantly, by a drunk driver." She glanced up, her eyes filling.

Hank knew better than anyone about car accidents, how a split second of bad luck could ruin your life. His scars began to throb and his stomach lurched as if he'd been punched hard.

"I'm real sorry," he said. Though he didn't get why her cousin's death screwed up her life.

"Thanks." She blinked away the tears. "She was my only living relative. I wish we'd spent more time together." She stared past him at something only she could see.

So she had nobody. Hank wondered what that felt like. He came from a large family, most of them still living in the Seattle area. Since the accident, not needing or wanting their sympathy, he rarely talked to them and only saw them on holidays. But he knew they were there.

"Is that why you're heading to Bellingham, for the funeral?" he asked.

"Partly, but it's more complicated than that. Rosanne left something behind, something I need to pick up." She hugged her waist, then, as if unable to sit still, jumped up. "I'd better check on those pills."

"She left you something, eh? That doesn't sound so bad," Hank pressed, against his better judgment.

She'd suckered him in with her pale face and sad story. Unwilling to let her go without further explanation and unable to fathom what had her spooked, he raised his brow in question.

"Oh, no?" Her hand stilled on the doorknob. The eyes that met his were more apprehensive than sorrowful. "This is no ordinary inheritance. She left me her three-week-old son."

Chapter Three

Mia locked her icy hands in her lap while the forty-something Judith Ellison, who preferred to be called by her first name, pored through documents in the folder atop her large mahogany desk. Beginning with the funeral two days ago, it had been an emotional few days, and Mia longed to return to Forest Glen and her work. At least Sookie was there, looking after the hawk and other animals too sick to leave the clinic.

Nodding to herself, Judith slipped on her rimless glasses and jotted down notes, leaving Mia to her thoughts. Mia shifted in her seat and avoided looking at the infant ensconced in the baby carrier on the carpet beside her. Thankfully, he was asleep.

However she was wide awake, her nerves on edge and her stomach in knots. A dull throbbing had started behind her eyes, signaling a stress headache. Resisting the urge to glance at the baby she pulled in a calming breath, which did no good at all, and studied the attorney's brunette chignon, a feminine touch amid the crisp white blouse and expensive tailored suit. The woman seemed both competent and friendly. It was clear why Rosanne had hired her.

"Are you sure Drew's father doesn't want him?" Mia asked. "I mean, I know he didn't make it to the funeral, but…"

Judith set down her pen and shook her head. "I have Mr. Wilkins's signed, notarized waiver relinquishing any and all rights to parenthood. His parents are too elderly and frail to take the boy, nor do they have an interest in their grandson."

"Surely some other relative will want him," Mia pressed.

The attorney eyed her over the tops of her glasses. "There are none."

Mia nodded to show she understood. Poor, dear little Drew. He'd lost his mother, and his father didn't want him. Now he was stuck with her, at least for a while.

"Let's sum up our discussion, shall we?" Judith scanned the notes on her yellow legal pad. "First, as legal guardian of Andrew Mathis, you are responsible for providing the boy a home. Second, you have first rights to adoption after a home visit and certification by a social worker. Third, you have opted against those rights but you agree to care for Andrew until suitable parents are found. Fourth, you will make the final decision as to Andrew's permanent family." She glanced at Mia. "Do I have that right?"

"Yes," Mia replied in a small voice.

The older woman leaned halfway across the desk to peer at the baby. Her prim mouth softened before she returned her attention to Mia. "You're certain about giving him up?" she asked, her gaze direct and without even a touch of censure.

Regardless, Mia couldn't help but feel as if she were being judged. The knots in her stomach tightened and her head began to pound. Yet she knew her decision was best for the baby. This time she nodded vigorously. "I am."

Judith jotted a notation on the already crowded sheet of paper and added it to the folder. "If you have no objection, I'll make the referral to a private adoption agency I often use. They'll be in touch." She pushed her glasses atop her head.

"When should I expect to hear from them?"

"I can't say for certain, but since Drew is a healthy, Caucasian baby and there aren't many of those available for adoption, it'll likely be fast. The agency may select several families and ask you to choose one—leaving out identifying factors such as the last name, of course. Be assured that every couple is carefully screened in advance and must pass a thorough background check and show financial solvency. Their homes are visited and evaluated by qualified social workers. Once you choose, should you wish, you'll have the chance to meet Andrew's prospective parents."

"That's good to know."

Drew made a funny, gurgling sound. Mia's attention darted to him. Wonder filled her as it did whenever she looked at him. He was so tiny and so perfect. His eyes were closed, but she could see movement behind the thin eyelids. He must be dreaming, she thought, studying the fluffy, near-black fuzz on his little, round head. Talking in his sleep.

A dim memory from long ago popped into her mind, of her mother's laughter when Mia had talked in her sleep.

The collar on his blue cotton sweater had ridden up, rubbing against his cheek. Leaning down, she smoothed the fabric flat with unsteady fingers. The back of her hand touched the incredibly soft skin of his plump baby cheek. His rosebud mouth puckered as if suckling, then relaxed in its open-mouthed sleep position.

Judith chuckled, professionalism forgotten for the moment. "They're so helpless and innocent at that age, totally dependent on you."

She was only making conversation, but the words stung like a slap. All the more reason Drew needed someone else to mother him. Mia snatched back her hand and sat up straight.

The woman across the desk didn't seem to notice her distress. "I remember when mine were little. I was nervous, too, just like you."

Not like me at all. But Mia wasn't about to tell this stranger her dark secret.

"With time and experience, you gain confidence and things get easier. You know, you can change your mind about the adoption, right up until you sign the final papers."

Mia couldn't fathom a reply. The attorney seemed to think her decision to give up Drew stemmed from inexperience. Though the situation wasn't funny, she had a sudden urge to laugh hysterically. She stifled it and ended up yawning.

Judith's mouth quirked. "So he kept you up last night."

Now that was something Mia could discuss openly. "He did," she said. "He seems to sleep better during the day."

"Both my daughters slept soundly from the beginning, thank goodness. I don't envy you those sleepless nights." The intercom buzzed. "This is a call I need to take. Would you mind stepping outside for a moment?" With an apologetic smile, the attorney slid a fresh notepad from a side drawer, slipped on her glasses, then lifted the phone.

Mia rose and carefully toted Drew into the plush hallway. She set down the carrier and looked away, wishing she could trust Judith and explain her reservations. Heaven knew it would be a relief to talk to someone. But having carried her secret for such a long time, she feared sharing it.

Yet from the moment she'd learned about Drew, the urge to open up had grown, until the other day when she'd considered confiding in Hank. Who knew why. Possibly because he'd sensed her turmoil and asked about it, his eyes intent on her as if she really mattered. She recalled the concern in his voice, his hands warm and solid on her shoulders as he guided her to a chair.

Her heart stuttered at the memory. She couldn't remember the last time a man had worried about her, let alone touched her. Mia frowned. Was she so hungry for a man's touch that she'd pour out her troubles as payment?

No, she assured herself. Absolutely not. This whole situation had surprised and shocked her so much that she wasn't herself. Hank happened to be there with a ready ear, his willingness to listen an enticement to speak. In the end though, she'd held fast to her horrible secret, had simply told him what the whole town would know by lunchtime. Forest Glen might be sparsely populated, but news traveled through it with the speed of lightning.

Everybody knew about her cousin and Drew, but no one had guessed that under Mia's care, bad things could happen.

Drew might get sick. He might even die.

Like Gracie.

Dear God, no. Mia swallowed hard, her throat tight with emotion. She was grateful to be standing unobserved in the hallway.

Badly in need of distraction, she stared at the oil painting on the wall. A peaceful boat on a calm sea, she noted without really seeing it. *Gracie.* Long ago Mia had determined never to forget her little sister, and rarely a day went by without thinking of her. She bowed her head and squeezed her eyes shut. Gracie Louise Barker would be twenty-four now. Would she have been smart? Pretty? Probably both, a lovely woman with children of her own. Since she had only lived three short months, there was no way of knowing.

Drew made another funny sound and Mia turned her attention to him. Talking in his sleep again. A smile tugged her mouth.

Gracie had been only a couple of months older than Drew when she died. What if the same thing happened to him? The smile vanished. Fear and panic turned her stomach, and bile rose in her throat. About to lose the little breakfast she'd eaten, she hastily returned to Judith's office.

"Would you watch Drew while I use the rest-room?" she said, not caring that she disrupted the attorney's call.

The woman glanced up. "Go ahead," she mouthed.

Mia hurried from the room. Moving blindly and silently across the thick hallway carpet, she dashed into the restroom. Mercifully it was empty save for her.

Feeling more scared than sick she rushed into a stall. Only after the door was bolted did she let loose the memory that haunted her.

SHE WAS FIVE years old, "watching" three-month-old Gracie while her mother showered. Her father had left for work. Mia felt so grown up and responsible. She wanted Gracie to be happy, so she got her Baby-Wets-A-Lot. She dragged a chair to the crib and climbed onto it. Now she could easily reach Gracie. She placed her beloved doll beside her sister, who lay quietly on her tummy.

Mia tapped her on the shoulder. "I'm letting you play with my dolly, but you can't spit up on her."

Gracie didn't move. She didn't wake up or make noises or cry. Puzzled, Mia frowned at her. Mommy would know what to do. But her mother didn't like to be bothered when she was in the bathroom. Mia sat down with her coloring book and crayons and waited until her mother came.

It seemed like forever, but Mommy finally walked into the baby's room. She looked into the bed, gasped, then screamed.

Mia glanced up in alarm. "What's the matter, Mommy?"

"Not now, Mia."

Her mother ran to the phone. An ambulance came. After that, Mommy cried and cried. She didn't pay any attention to Mia for a long time.

Mia knew she'd done something very bad. She just didn't know what it was.

THE MEMORY FADED in an anguished cry, followed by a flood of tears. It had happened a long time ago. She didn't know why she needed to cry anymore than she knew why her heart felt bruised.

Finally the tears stopped. She blew her nose, then unbolted the door. Standing at the sink, she splashed cool water over her face. She blotted her skin dry with a paper towel, then studied herself in the mirror. Grief, guilt, worry and lack of sleep had taken their tolls, and purple shadows stained the skin beneath her eyes. She'd even lost weight, looked almost gaunt.

Straightening her shoulders, she made a silent vow. She must do what was best for Drew—find a nice couple to adopt him, loving parents to keep him safe. The sooner, the better.

Before it was too late.

HANK WAITED until the crew broke for lunch on Thursday before he brought Nugget to Mia's for his checkup. It was her first day back and a beautiful spring day. According to Sookie she had a full morning scheduled, but after lunch things were slow enough that he and Nugget could drop in anytime.

Although favoring his sore foot slowed his usual fast trot to an awkward lope, Nugget was getting around on his own.

Birds chirped merrily and the warm sun brightened the way across the uneven meadow and stand of madronas. The closer they came to the cabin, the faster Nugget's tail wagged. Hank, too, looked forward to seeing Mia, with a strange exhilaration that lit him up inside. That thought stopped him cold.

"She's your vet," he muttered to the dog. "That's the only reason for this visit, so don't go getting any ideas."

Nugget cocked his head and stared at him as if to say, "Yeah, right."

"Okay," Hank admitted. "I want to know about the funeral." And see how she was doing with the baby.

For days his crew had buzzed with the sad news of Mia's dead cousin and the infant boy left behind. From what Hank had learned, most of his men had gone through grade school and high school with her.

A few even had dated her. She'd moved to Forest Glen around age five, to be raised by her grandmother in the cabin where she now lived. She must have lost her parents at a young age, which was a shame. Word had it she was really nervous about this baby and that she planned to keep him only until an agency found people to adopt him.

With the dog at his side, he headed up the earthen path to the door. He tried the knob, but the damn thing was locked, as it had been last time he was here. The Closed sign stood in the window, with Back At One O'clock hand lettered in black marker beneath it. With a baby, he guessed she needed some time away from the clinic.

He wouldn't see her, then. The sharp sting of disappointment seemed unwarranted for the situation, and he swore at himself as he turned to go.

"We'll come back another time," he muttered.

As he and Nugget started back down the path, they heard a baby's lusty cry. The dog's ears flicked forward and he slanted his head quizzically at the sound.

"That's the little baby," Hank said. "Drew."

The wailing intensified, the nonstop, anguished cries knifing straight into him. He didn't stop to think, just strode around the house to the back. Mia had planted a flower garden along the south side. Daffodils, red tulips and purple primroses waved cheerily at him as he hurried past. He wiped his feet on the mat at the back door, noting the three old-fashioned breaker panels near the window. Old wiring like that could be dangerous. He'd tell Mia, suggest she update. He knocked but no one answered. The kitchen door wasn't locked, so he walked in.

The baby's cries filled the room and Hank forgot about the wiring. Sookie was nowhere in sight. Ginger and the tomcat were huddled together on their mattress, shooting worried glances toward a battered rocking chair where Mia cradled a squirming bundle while rocking rapidly back and forth. She didn't even ask Hank why he'd entered without knocking, just shot him a panicked look.

"Drew won't stop crying, and I don't know what to do."

"Did you try feeding him?" he asked as Nugget slunk toward the other animals. Dropping down beside Ginger, he buried his head under his uninjured paw.

"Of course I did," she snapped. "Drew doesn't have a temperature or a rash. He's not acting sleepy. He ate a while ago and I just changed his diaper. I burped him several times, too. Nothing helps." She hung her head, looking thoroughly dejected.

Seeing her scared and distraught made Hank's chest hurt. He swore softly and considered turning around and leaving. This was not his problem.

He glanced around in desperation. "Where's Sookie?"

"At lunch. She's working full-time for me now, so she gets an hour." Mia sniffled and brushed her eyes with the back of her free hand. "Today she's taking extra time, since her wedding anniversary is tomorrow and she needed to go shopping. When she left, Drew was fine." She chewed her lip, as she seemed to do whenever she was distressed, while tears flooded her eyes. "What am I doing wrong, Hank?"

Now the baby and the woman were both bawling. Great, just great. Hank hated when women cried. He never knew what to do. Especially now, with Mia, a competent veterinarian who didn't seem the type to bawl at any little thing.

He scratched the back of his neck and shifted uncomfortably. "My guess is you're not doing anything wrong. Poor kid probably has colic."

His words didn't seem to help. Mia still looked miserable and lost. Well, hell. Like it or not, he had to do something. He reached for the infant. "Give him to me."

As a testament to her mental state, she didn't question or argue with him, just nodded and obeyed.

The boy weighed nothing. His little arms and legs flailed and his cheeks were red from crying. Poor little tyke. A wave of tenderness rushed over Hank.

He hadn't handled a baby in a while, but that wasn't something a man forgot how to do. He cradled the tiny, warm body high up on his chest, positioning Drew's head at the crook of his shoulder so he could look around.

Holding the boy reminded him of his niece and nephew, and that reminded him of his sister, Lisa, and Ryan, her husband. And his big brother, Jake. He hadn't seen any of them since Christmas. He missed them, he realized with a pang. But now was no time to think about that.

He began a song that had worked to calm his sister's babies. "Hush little baby, don't you cry..."

The wailing stopped, but only for a moment. Hank barely had time to heave a relieved breath before the kid started up again, his little body stiff and vibrating with the effort. Continuing the song, he paced slowly and gently patted Drew's back.

After a few seconds the bawling stopped for good. Drew hiccuped deep breaths that shook his body, but stayed quiet.

In the sudden silence, Nugget lifted his head, Ginger wagged her tail and Rags began to purr, sounding like an idling engine.

Mia's jaw dropped. "How did you do that?"

"Experience." Hank shrugged. "My sister has kids. Both of them had colic. Walking seems to help, or taking a drive in the car."

Mia groaned. "Looks like I'll be getting my exercise." She hesitated. "Is colic dangerous? Could a baby with colic," she swallowed hard, "die?"

What had made her think that? Hank shook his head. "Hardly. Both my sister's kids had trouble digesting cow's milk. The doctor put them on soy formula, and that did the trick. If I were you, I'd ask the pediatrician about that."

"I will." Some of the tension eased from her posture and she settled more comfortably into the rocker. "We have a doctor's appointment first thing tomorrow."

Hank nodded. "He'll know what to do." He glanced down at the bundle against his chest. Sober blue-gray eyes studied him. Hank smiled and touched the soft, fuzzy head. "He sure is a cute little thing."

"Except when he cries." Mia shoved her hair, which looked as if she'd forgotten to comb it, behind her ears and tucked one leg beneath her. "What a set of lungs."

Hank watched her other foot push the rocker in a slow, even rhythm. She wore no makeup. A smudge stained her cheek, from the tears or something else, and she wore a loose white blouse and her usual black slacks. Nothing attractive about it, but his body disagreed.

He wanted to lean down and kiss that smudge, then kiss the worried frown from her lips.

And what then? What if she let him? He'd want more, and sooner or later she might, too. He wasn't about to set himself up for the humiliation that would surely follow. He decided it was best to ignore his feelings.

"I noticed three breaker panels outside. Your wiring looks old and probably isn't up to code. You ought to update it. Oh, and your gutters could stand cleaning."

"I know, and I keep meaning to clean them," she said. "As for the wiring, you're not the first person to mention what a mess it is. Seems like Sookie and I blow fuses several times a month. I should have updated it when I added on the clinic, but I didn't want to spend the money." Some of her hair had fallen into her eyes and she blew it back. "Like the gutters, it's on my list of things to do." She glanced at the baby in his arms. "If I ever get a minute to myself."

"Babies sure do take up your time. Aside from that and the colic, how do you like motherhood?"

The rocking stopped, and a look of shock came over her face, as if he'd called her a dirty word. She sat up straight and planted both feet on the floor.

"I am not Drew's mother," she stated in a jittery voice a pitch higher than usual.

Apparently he'd hit a sore spot. He raised his eyebrows in question, but one look at the flash in her eyes—was it anger or fear?—and he decided not to ask.

"Excuse me. I meant legal guardian. You really ought to relax though, because when you're tense, he knows it. That only makes things worse."

"Thank you, Doctor Adams." Her eyes narrowed, not in hostility, but as if she'd finally realized he was standing in her kitchen. "What exactly are you doing here?"

Hank stopped pacing and thrust his chin toward his dog. "You said to bring Nugget by today." At her blank look he added, "To check his paw."

"That's right." Mia smacked her forehead with the heel of her hand. For the first time, she glanced at the animals. "I didn't mean to forget you, Nugget." She offered the dog a watery smile that softened and brightened her face and made her look astonishingly pretty. "Things have been all turned around since Drew arrived." She stood and reached for the baby.

As Hank lifted him from his chest, the infant let out a sound of distress. Her eyes widened in panic. "If you'll keep Drew from crying, I'll check Nugget's paw. No charge."

Hank couldn't have turned down that desperate offer if he'd wanted to. Also, he wanted that smile back. He nodded. "Fair enough."

The shadows faded from her eyes as she nodded gratefully. Quickly, she led Nugget from the room.

Hank's gaze dropped to her hips. Given her loose, untucked blouse, there wasn't much to see. But he looked anyway.

He caught her dog and cat watching him, and scowled. "You're as bad as Nugget. Don't go getting any ideas. The minute she finishes that checkup, I'm out of here."

Drew squirmed and made a soft sound. "Tired of being on my shoulder, eh?" Hank shifted the kid from his chest to the crook of his arm. Big baby eyes studied him again, while one tiny hand grasped his index finger and held on with surprising strength. Then the miraculous happened: Drew's round mouth lifted at the corners. Was that a smile? A sweet warmth blossomed and spread through Hank's chest. He chuckled, cooing at the infant like a silly fool.

Catching himself, he swore softly. He slid his finger from the tiny grasp and returned the baby to his shoulder. "Uh-uh, squirt. I don't have time to get involved with you." Or Mia.

He had a house to build and a life to live, and his plans didn't include a woman or a baby.

Mia and Drew were temporary neighbors, period.

Chapter Four

Late Friday afternoon Hank stood at his trailer's kitchen sink, freshly showered and relishing the silence. As badly as he wanted to finish building the house, he needed a break. Besides, he and the crew had put in a long, grueling week. Everybody needed the weekend to recuperate.

After they'd left, Hank had wanted to keep working, but his hip and back bothered him. Actually, they hurt like a son of a bitch. It had been close to two years since the accident. How much longer before his body regained its full strength? Sometimes he wondered whether it ever would.

If his muscles stayed weak and hurt forever, well then, he'd accept the pain as his due—small penance for his sins. For one brief moment his thoughts turned dark. But he wouldn't go there.

Though he rubbed the small of his back, his strained muscles continued to throb.

What he wouldn't give for a Scotch, neat…. But he'd given up alcohol after the accident. So he filled a glass with water and downed two pain tablets. Swiping his mouth with the back of his hand, he stood at the window, which afforded him an obstructed view of the house, or what there was of it so far. A chain-link fence stood around the perimeter of the site. Inside were the cement foundation, a week's worth of framing, mounds of dirt and muddy equipment.

To the untrained eye it didn't look like much. But Hank could see the finished product as clear as the scale model replica in his living room/office.

On a whim he grabbed a kitchen chair and hauled it through the door and down the fold-up, metal front steps. After the cold snap earlier in the week the temperature had steadily climbed, and today had been mild and sunny. Even now with the sun starting its descent the air remained unseasonably warm. He placed the chair on the packed dirt, facing the project and, grimacing, lowered himself onto it.

Though it would take a good week to complete the framing, things were right on schedule. That felt good. He took a deep, relaxing breath, inhaling the scents of plowed earth, spring grass and flowers. Nothing he hadn't smelled before, but stronger and richer here in the country. No wonder Gil—his partner—had loved the area.

Nugget settled down on the lone patch of grass beside Hank, propping his head on his paws without hesitation. Thanks to Mia's skilled stitching job and the antibiotics, his injury was healing nicely.

With both dog and machines silent, sounds from the woods filled the air. Hank heard the gurgling stream at the far side of the property. Dozens of birds high in the trees called back and forth, and a pair of chunky, brown squirrels chattered playfully as they darted up a huge pine. He envied them their carefree existence.

His ambitious plans kept him far too busy for play. Yes, he could take a few days off, probably should to rest his battered body. But he knew he'd be up at dawn tomorrow, working alone on the small things that didn't require a team. Tonight though, once the pain pills kicked in, he intended to enjoy the solitude and relax with a good mystery novel. Until then, he'd focus on the barely started house, using his architect's training to visualize the end result.

Without a doubt this would be the most fluid, beautiful home he'd ever built. Gil had designed the place shortly before the accident that had cost him his life. Four months ago Hank had discovered the plans stuffed under a pile of old blueprints. He'd put everything on hold to build the structure just as Gil had designed it.

The clean lines and light, airy feeling of the house

surrounded by woods and stream was sure to win the Architectural Award of the West. When he won, Hank planned to dedicate the award to Gil. He felt good just thinking about that, certain Gil would approve. It was the least he could do. Maybe then the guilt would ease up.

Right, and there was gold at the end of the rainbow. Hank snickered. Nugget raised his head and shot him a puzzled look.

"Go back to sleep, mutt." He scratched the dog's head.

No award could atone for the accident. He wished he could go back and relive that night, wished he hadn't celebrated the finish of the huge, expensive waterfront house with one too many drinks. That he'd been sober enough to drive home instead of handing Gil the keys. If Hank had been at the wheel, he might have taken a different route where no truck would cross the line and plow into the driver's side of the Jeep. Gil would be alive. Hank would have no pain or hideous scars on his hip, belly and back to send Kristin running. They even might be married with a couple of kids.

Longing hit him hard. Not for Kristin—he was over her—but because he'd always imagined himself a husband and father. He shook his head in regret. There was no way to change the past. And anyway, as things were, he was better off alone.

White-hot pain burned his back and hip muscles.

The pain reliever sure was taking its time. "Relax," he ordered out loud.

He rolled his shoulders, closed his eyes and let his mind wander. His thoughts went straight to yesterday, to Mia. Insisting she wasn't Drew's mother, yet as concerned and upset as any mother.

The amazing thing was, she'd trusted him with Drew. Hank's throat tightened with emotion, for it had been a while since a woman had needed and trusted him. He hadn't realized how much he missed that. Maybe he and Mia—

His eyes snapped open. Uh-uh, he wasn't going there, wasn't getting involved. His jaw set in resolve. Yet he couldn't help wondering how she'd managed today, how the doctor's appointment went and whether Drew had colic or something else.

As if his thoughts had summoned her, Mia emerged from between two tall madronas, with Drew strapped to her chest and Ginger on a ten-foot leash. They headed toward Hank.

He groaned. Given the unwanted turn of his thoughts, she was the last person he wanted to see. Yet at the same time, anticipation lifted his spirits. She'd made no secret that she didn't like him tearing up the land abutting hers, and had never visited the site. He puffed with pride that she'd see what he'd accomplished and what he planned. Maybe if she understood what he was building, she'd accept it.

Her hands cupped around the navy canvas baby carrier that was fat and rounded with Drew, she picked her way across the spring grass, moving slowly toward Hank. A fanny pack bounced on her hip, yet despite the uneven weight caused by it and the baby, her movements were fluid and graceful. Her loose black slacks stretched across her thighs with each step. Nothing suggestive or sexy, but enough to reveal her slenderness.

When a sliver of setting sun struck her head and shoulders, her flighty, light brown hair shone like polished bronze. The exertion of walking over the uneven ground with the unfamiliar weight of a baby had tinted her pale cheeks rosy, and her full, bare lips were parted unselfconsciously.

Hank thought her the most beautiful woman he'd ever seen, and that irritated him. She was off-limits. He wanted her to go away, but the manners his mother had long ago drilled into him kicked in. He pushed to his feet, but couldn't wipe the unwelcoming scowl from his face. He opened the gate of the chain-link fence and, settling his hands low on his hips, waited for her.

HANK'S UNFRIENDLY expression caught Mia by surprise. He didn't want her here.

Stiffening, she backed up a step. "Looks like I'm bothering you. Sorry." She tugged on the leash.

"Come on, Ginger." Tossing a reluctant look at Nugget, the three-legged canine moved to Mia's side. She pivoted toward the madronas.

"Wait," Hank called in a commanding tone she couldn't ignore.

She sighed and turned toward him. "Why? I get the message—you don't want us here."

"You caught me off guard," he said. "I parked my trailer here three weeks ago and this is the first time you've visited. In fact you made it clear that you disapprove of what I'm doing." He gestured at the churned earth and construction.

"I still do." Prickling heat climbed her neck and face, as it often did when she was angry. But this was no time to pick a fight. She didn't have the energy, and certainly didn't want to go home. That meant being alone with Drew, and *that* scared her.

Hank seemed to know what to do around babies. She needed him. Of course her pride wouldn't let her admit that. "But I'm not here to argue." She forced a friendly tone. "It's a nice afternoon, and since staying on the move keeps Drew happy, I thought I'd walk over and thank you for helping me yesterday."

"No problem."

Warmth flared in Hank's eyes, banked and gone so quickly, she thought she'd imagined it. Nugget nudged his snout against his master's thigh. Hank scratched between the dog's ears. Then he opened the gate of a large dog run beside the fenced con-struction site. "I put this up the other day, to keep Nugget from exploring and getting hurt again."

"I approve," Mia said.

Nugget and Ginger yipped and Mia unleashed the dog. The animals scampered into the pen, sniffing with enthusiasm.

Hank latched the gate, then shifted his weight, wincing. Face laced with pain, he massaged his lower back. "How'd the doctor's appointment go?"

Mia knew how to work kinks from muscles, at least on animals. But she didn't know Hank well enough to offer her services. It seemed too intimate.

"Dr. Sweeney agrees with you," she said, patting the baby's little back. "Drew has colic. It's nothing fatal," she said, her happiness over that news coloring her voice. For now, the baby was safe. "He suggested the same things you did," she added, rocking her upper body to keep the infant content. "Walking Drew around and switching to soy milk."

Hank nodded soberly. "Thought he might," he said, studying her face.

What did he see there? Suddenly self-conscious, Mia wished she'd changed her clothes and stopped to comb her hair and apply lip gloss. But with Drew taking up every minute of her time, she simply hadn't thought beyond his next feeding or diaper change.

Besides, this was Hank Adams. He was no more interested in her than she was in him. "As long as I'm on the move, Drew's quiet. The second I stop, he cries. We started the soy milk tonight. I sure hope it helps."

"He'll let you know." Hank's expression mellowed as he glanced at Drew.

"Can you see his face?" She turned sideways and held the Snugli open. "Is he asleep?"

He moved closer and peered at the baby. "Hard to tell," he said, nudging Mia's hand aside with his own.

The casual touch zinged through her, setting her jagged nerves further on edge and all but erasing her fatigue. She heard Hank's swift intake of breath. He jerked his hand back and kept his attention on the baby.

"Yeah, he's asleep," he said in a brusque tone.

As he straightened, she caught a whiff of pine soap. She'd always loved the smell of that soap. She wanted to lean forward, bury her nose in the crook of Hank's sun-browned neck and breathe in his scent.

"Mmm," she murmured, hardly aware she'd made a sound.

"What?"

Goodness, what was she doing? If Hank knew what she was fantasizing…

"Nothing." Embarrassed and uncomfortable, she racked her brain for something to talk about. "I'm glad the clinic is closed over the weekend," she finally said. "I'll be able to rest when Drew does." She yawned and stretched her arms over her head. "At the moment I crave sleep more than anything."

"Anything?"

Hank's brow lifted suggestively and his mouth quirked. His gaze locked on hers, the bright heat in his golden eyes unmistakable. Maybe he *did* read minds.

By the heat scalding her cheeks, Mia knew she was blushing. A dark flush bloomed on Hank's ears before he turned away. Mia had never known a man whose ears blushed. She stifled a smile.

He'd never teased her before. Not sure how to react, she pretended to straighten her fanny pack.

Hank nodded toward the construction. "As long as you're here, I may as well show you around."

She surveyed the stacks of lumber, mounds of dirt and the large, rudimentary frame where Doc's cabin and half of the meadow used to sit. "I can see just fine," she said without bothering to hide her disapproval.

"What do you have against me?"

With his hands low on his hips and his eyes narrowed, he was almost scary. Mia refused to let him intimidate her. She met his gaze straight on.

"You're a builder. You plow up the woods along with the homes of countless wild animals, without a thought about anything but making a profit. Thanks to careless people like you, I'm rehabilitating my second wild bird this spring." Her voice had grown louder as she spoke. She stopped abruptly and glanced down at Drew, who luckily remained quiet and still. "Those are the main reasons," she finished in a softer voice.

Hank winced. "That's harsh."

"Well, you asked." She waved a hand at the mess before them. "The proof of my words is right here."

Shaking his head, he muttered something about patience. "If you'd bothered to ask, you'd know I haven't cut down a single tree. I only disturbed what I had to. There's a scale model of the house inside, including the grounds. You ought to take a look at it. You just might change your opinion."

Despite herself Mia wanted to see what the finished product would look like. But going inside the trailer where Hank lived seemed too personal.

He didn't await her reply, simply climbed the front steps as if assuming she'd follow. She couldn't help admiring his long, broad back, noting the play of muscles under his black T-shirt. And the muscles didn't stop there. His biceps were as well developed as any weight lifter's; only honest, physical labor had defined and toned him.

The man had a body to die for, and smelled good, too.

Desire flared low in her belly, unwanted and confusing. She frowned. She hadn't thought about sex in a long time, yet here she was, body humming and mind fixated on the subject. Wanting a man she hardly knew, with a baby strapped to her chest. Either she was crazy or her sleep deprivation was more serious than she'd thought. Or both.

Hank opened the door, pausing to glance at her over his shoulder. "Coming?"

A few minutes inside couldn't hurt. She'd look at the model, then leave.

"Why not?" She followed him up the steps.

WITH SMALL WINDOWS and heavy curtains, Hank's trailer was quite a bit darker than the waning daylight outdoors. He flicked on a lamp while Mia's gaze circled his living room/office.

No doubt she found the white walls, brown carpet and beige sofa as drab as her cabin was colorful.

"The model's over there." He gestured toward the drafting table that took up a full corner of the room, then headed to the sofa where he usually ate his meals. The plate and glass he'd used for his early dinner of frozen pizza were still on the coffee table. She'd think him a slob, and for some reason he didn't want that. He carried them into the compact kitchen a short distance away.

When he returned to the room she was walking slowly around the model. "You really plan to restore the grounds the way you've shown here?"

"Exactly as you see it," he assured her.

She nodded thoughtfully. "This is much less intrusive than I imagined. The combination of wood and glass fits well with the woods. It's beautiful." She rewarded him with a smile. "You're a talented man."

Much as Hank wanted to take the credit, he couldn't. Standing beside her, he shook his head. "I didn't design the place. My former partner did."

"Former?" She shot him a curious look.

He hesitated, wondering how much to tell her. Then again, what had happened was no secret. "A man driving a truck fell asleep at the wheel. The truck crossed the line and crashed into the car. Gil died. Like what happened with your cousin."

Though he didn't flinch from her assessing gaze, he wanted to.

She blew out a sympathetic breath. "Oh, man, that's rough."

She didn't know the half of it.

She touched his arm in a gesture of comfort, but said nothing more. None of the shallow platitudes or awkward condolences people generally uttered. He appreciated that.

It seemed forever since a woman had touched him. He was keenly aware of her hand on his forearm, and of the desire stirring his body. He cleared his throat, which had gone dry. "It happened nearly two years ago. It's not as hard to bear now as it was."

"I don't think a person ever gets over the death of a loved one. At least—" she paused, blinking "—in my experience."

"That's right, you've lost everyone in your family. Except Drew."

A haunted look crossed her face. "Except Drew," she repeated, withdrawing her hand.

Hank mourned the loss of her touch. And though he wanted to know more, he didn't press her.

"He'll be gone as soon as the adoption agency finds the right family," she said.

The baby made noises. Head bowed, Mia hugged him and rocked from side to side. To comfort him, or herself?

She returned her attention to the model. "Gil designed something special. I can see why you want to build it. But this is a modern, sophisticated home. Why put it in Forest Glen, where we're anything but sophisticated? Surely there are more suitable lots in Seattle."

"He was an avid hiker," Hank explained. "He used to explore around here, and this is where he wanted the house."

She absorbed that with a brief nod. "Bart says you plan to enter some kind of competition?"

"The Architectural Award of the West. I stand a good chance of winning, and when I do, I'll dedicate the award to Gil. My way of honoring him."

She stopped rocking and nodded. An unfamiliar expression shone from her gaze. Respect, he thought, maybe admiration. He had to know. "Well, am I still the bad guy?"

"Not so bad." She smiled. "I owe you an apology. I'm sorry I've been so rude about all this." She waved her hand at the model.

The words rang sweet in his ears. He dipped his chin. "Accepted."

"Friends?" She held out her hand.

Following the accident he'd shut his friends out of his life. He didn't want friends.

Nevertheless, when Mia's eyes locked on his, he took her hand and shook. "Friends."

Warmth from her grip filled his whole body. He held on longer than necessary. Her eyes widened, then darkened, signaling interest. Responding hunger kindled in his belly. He wanted to pull her close and sink into her softness, bury his pain in the pleasuring of her.

No. Abruptly, he dropped her hand and backed away.

Red-faced, Mia averted her gaze and touched

her fingers to her lips. "All of a sudden I don't feel so good."

She looked shaky, as if she'd keel over any moment, the deep shadows under her eyes attesting to her exhaustion. Alarmed, Hank cupped her arm to guide her toward the sofa. "You should sit down."

"I'll be okay," she protested, digging her heels into the carpet. "I don't want to disturb Drew."

Hank peered at the baby, whose head was burrowed against Mia's chest. Lucky kid. "From what I can see, he's out cold."

"Thank heavens." She sighed wearily, unbuckled the fanny pack, and set it on the coffee table.

Hank eyed the swollen pack, with the snaps about to pop open. "That thing looks like it weighs ten pounds. What's in there?"

"A blanket, two bottles and a couple of diapers and clean clothes in case Drew needs something while we're out."

Spoken like a caring mother. He would have voiced the thought but, remembering Mia's hostile reaction last time they'd discussed motherhood, wisely refrained. "You want a cup of coffee? It's instant."

"Since I usually drink tea, I won't know the difference." Her mouth lifted into a weary smile. "If it has caffeine, I'll take it."

Hank fought the urge to help as she carefully

slipped the straps of the baby carrier from her shoulders. Touching her was dangerous. With tenderness she laid Drew on his back on the cushion of the sofa. She unsnapped the fabric between the leg holes and slowly eased the carrier over his head, her mouth skewed in concentration. The baby, dressed in a fuzzy green sleeper decorated with yellow elephants, slept on.

Mia sank down beside him, fixing him with an anxious look.

"You can relax now," Hank said.

Her mouth went tight with worry. "What if something goes wrong?"

"Hey, I'm an experienced uncle. I know about babies, remember? The kid's asleep. Nothing's going to bother him." He gave her an encouraging nod.

After a brief hesitation she sighed. "I hope you're right."

Unzipping the fanny pack, she found the baby blanket and opened it. Her eyes were warm and her face lit with tenderness as she covered the tiny torso. Yawning, she stretched and sat back. "Sweet dreams, little Drew. I hope, I hope." She crossed her fingers.

Hank waited until she lolled against the sofa back, her hand close to the baby's side, before heading into the kitchen. When he returned five minutes later with two coffees, she was asleep.

Well, well. She looked so tired, he couldn't disturb her. He got rid of the mugs, then retrieved a comforter and extra blanket from his bed. He spread the comforter over the floor. With great care he moved the slumbering Drew and his blanket onto it.

Next he untied and removed Mia's ankle boots. She sighed and stretched out on the sofa. Hank draped the extra blanket over her and her brow wrinkled. Hardly aware of his actions, he sank heavily onto the coffee table, leaned down and soothed his hand over the furrows. Her forehead smoothed out. The skin was as soft as he'd imagined, as soft as the baby's. The faint scent of baby powder and woman tickled his senses.

Feelings he didn't understand clogged his throat, and he swallowed thickly. He knew he should drop his hand, stand up and head the hell outside. Yet he couldn't seem to move, couldn't pull his gaze from Mia's face. Of their own volition, his fingers trailed gently down her pale, smooth cheek.

Her thick brown eyelashes fluttered against her pale skin. Eyes still closed, she turned her face into his hand, then touched her lips to the hard callus on his palm.

Hank's eyelids lowered to half-mast as sensations pulsed through his hand and arm to the rest of his body at warp speed—sharp heat and a driving hunger that would have brought him to his knees had he not been sitting down.

He barely stifled a groan. God help him, he had to taste that mouth. Both hands trembled as he cupped her face and gently raised her chin. He touched his lips to hers. Sweet, so sweet...

"Hank?" Her eyes opened, but her blank look told him she was still asleep.

He swore softly and quickly straightened. "Everything's fine," he murmured, releasing her.

"Mmm, good." Her eyelids fluttered shut.

He let out a relieved breath, then glanced at the erection straining his jeans. He frowned. What in hell had just happened? The woman was totally out of it, for God's sake, and yet he'd kissed her. She was beat and probably wouldn't remember. He hoped she wouldn't, because he didn't want to try to explain what he barely understood.

His hands curled into frustrated fists. *Fool.*

Muscles aching, he lowered himself awkwardly to the floor. He shoved the coffee table aside. Bit by bit, he inched over, grimacing at the pull in his hip, until the sofa provided a backrest for him and the slumbering baby was within reach.

They slept like a matched pair, mother and son. For Mia *was* Drew's mother, whether or not she admitted it. Hank didn't believe she'd give up the boy. He wondered why she wanted to, but he didn't have the right to ask.

His mouth tightened. No, her troubles were none

of his concern. Even knowing that, frustration, desire and tenderness tangled up inside of him, along with the need to watch over and protect this woman and infant.

Now that was damn scary, not to mention stupid. He had no business feeling anything for Mia or Drew, and didn't want them here. But both were exhausted, and he didn't have the heart to wake them.

Outside, Nugget woofed, and Ginger answered. Good thing they were fenced in together. If they got cold they'd curl up in the doghouse, where Hank had placed a dog bed. He reached up and turned off the lamp. The light over the kitchen sink spilled softly into the room, creating deep shadows.

If he were smart he'd try to get some rest. He shook his head, knowing he wouldn't sleep as long as Drew and Mia were here. The hard floor was unforgiving to his sore back and hip, but he'd stay put and wait for one of them to wake up.

Until then he was trapped in his own living room.

Chapter Five

Mia opened her eyes, blinking in the dim light from...Hank's kitchen. The blanket covering her smelled like him and, groggy and disoriented, she breathed in his scent. She yawned and stretched. Her feet bumped the arm of the couch, gently prodding her awake. What in the world was she doing here? She must have fallen asleep but had no recollection of closing her eyes.

The last thing she remembered was laying Drew down and—*Drew.* Where was he?

Instantly awake, heart pounding, she jolted up, her eyes making a frantic search of the room. A large, blue comforter was folded on the floor. Beside it lay the unzipped fanny pack, and it was empty. There was no sign of Drew or Hank.

But she heard sounds, low, barely audible masculine murmurs from somewhere else in the trailer. She recognized the deep timbre of Hank's voice in song. The very thought made her smile, because he didn't strike her as the type to sing himself to sleep. He must be entertaining Drew.

She hadn't even heard the baby cry. Self-doubt erased the smile from her face. Didn't that just prove how unfit she was to be a mother? It certainly justified her decision to let some nice couple adopt Drew. Her heart twinged painfully at the thought. Suddenly she ached to hold and cuddle the baby.

She stood and nearly tripped over her boots, placed neatly on the floor near her feet. Again she drew a blank. Hank must have taken them off. Under his gruff ways, he was a thoughtful man. A good man.

In her socks she padded silently toward the sound of his voice, down a short, unadorned hall, past a small bathroom, to the lamp-lit room at the far end.

Hank's bedroom. He was singing "Baby Face," his rough bass voice slightly off-key. He'd sung to Drew the other day, too. Why it touched her so tonight, she didn't know. He was leaning against the headboard, legs stretched out and head angled toward the baby, who was devouring his bottle in loud gulps. He didn't see Mia, and she hovered uncertainly on the threshold, feeling as if she was spying on a private moment, yet reluctant to interrupt.

She knew she should collect Drew and go home,

but he was safer here with Hank watching over him. Maybe if she observed for a while she'd learn something. So she didn't announce her presence, just absorbed the scene.

Hank's bedroom looked like the other rooms in the trailer, its walls a stark, unadorned white. There were no photos or color, no homey touches anywhere. Only utilitarian blinds pulled against the night and a double bed containing a big, unshaved man in a T-shirt feeding a tiny baby in the crook of his arm. The picture they made together was so sweet, Mia's heart ached.

Hank was great with Drew. He'd make a wonderful father. Why wasn't he married with children? Sookie had mentioned that he was "a man with a past." Did that have something to do with why he was alone? Had some woman broken his heart?

All of a sudden a vivid dream she'd had tonight popped into her mind—that Hank had kissed her. It had seemed so real that she knew the feel of his hands on her face, right down to the calluses on his fingertips. She knew the teasing graze of his lips over hers, too light and too fast, but promising more.

Warmth stirred her blood and yearning blossomed low in her body. A longing moan slipped from her throat.

Clearly surprised, Hank shot his attention toward her. "You're awake."

His gaze swept over her, eyes hooded and mouth tight as if he were angry. He didn't want her.

Acute disappointment stabbed her heart. Better this way, she assured herself. With Drew to worry about she had neither the time nor the energy for a relationship. Besides, as soon as Hank finished the house he was heading back to Seattle.

"Sorry about falling asleep," she said. "Why didn't you wake me?"

"You needed the rest."

She noted the shadows under Hank's eyes and the weary lines around his mouth. "So do you."

The mundane conversation felt incredibly intimate. Maybe due to the late hour or because she was here in Hank's bedroom and he was dressed in the T-shirt and sweatpants he probably slept in every night.

Mia frowned at the tiny bundle cradled against his broad chest. "Has Drew cried much? If he did, I didn't hear it. He's kept you up, hasn't he?"

"I don't mind." Hank shrugged. "He hasn't bothered me except to eat. When he started to fuss I brought him in here so he wouldn't wake you."

No wonder she hadn't heard anything. She should have figured on Hank's thoughtfulness. Then she hadn't neglected the baby, after all. She let out a relieved breath.

"Thanks," she said, dipping her head. "That was very considerate of you."

His ears flushed red and he dropped his gaze to Drew, who had spit out the nipple. "No problem."

Milk dribbled down his little chin. Hank set the bottle on the bedside table, then wiped away the milk with his thumb. "I think the soy formula is working." He propped Drew on his shoulder and patted his back. "I've fed him twice. Both times he went right back to sleep."

"Twice?" Mia squinted at the clock near the bottle. "It can't be four in the morning. That means I slept nearly ten hours." She shook her head. "I never sleep that long."

"Guess you needed it." Hank's mouth quirked, making him look playful and incredibly attractive.

"Where are the dogs?"

"Where we left them, penned in the dog run. There's a mattress in the doghouse, and I figure they're keeping each other warm."

Keeping each other warm.

Suddenly Mia needed to escape the cozy scene. "I'll be right back."

The bathroom was so small she wondered how a big man like Hank maneuvered in it. Glancing in the mirror, she frowned at her reflection. The fatigue had vanished from her eyes but her skin was pale and her hair a tangled mess.

No wonder Hank wasn't attracted to her. She splashed warm water on her face and patted her skin dry with a neatly folded hand towel, then studied herself again. The water and towel had restored color to her skin. But her hair…

In search of a comb, she opened the cabinet. As long as it was open, may as well check out the contents. It wasn't nice to snoop, but the guilt that pricked her conscience didn't stop her. There were two metal shelves. The top held pain relievers, a box of bandages, antibacterial spray and razor blades. Deodorant, toothpaste, dental floss and a hairbrush crowded the bottom shelf. The usual items found in any bathroom.

Where were the condoms? Maybe in the bedside table drawer, or maybe he didn't have any. Or… Her face heated. What business was that of hers?

She picked up the brush and tugged it through her hair, wincing as it pulled through the snarls. Then she returned it to the cabinet and closed the door.

It was time to take Drew home. She retrieved the front pack from the living room. When she returned to Hank's bedroom, Drew was asleep on the bed, close to Hank's hip. Hank was still propped against the headboard, his head back and his eyes closed, his broad chest rising and falling in the relaxed rhythm of a man asleep. He must be exhausted.

Mia set the pack on the bed to settle Drew into it. Hank was less than an arm's length away. So close, she could see the black bristles of his morning beard.

Taking advantage of the moment, she boldly studied his broad shoulders and flat belly, plainly visible despite the loose T-shirt.

His long, muscled legs were stretched out in front of him. He had big feet and long toes. She followed the arch of his foot to his thick ankle, which was partly shrouded by the sweatpants. Her gaze swept upward, to the healthy bulge of his groin. What was that saying about big feet, big—

Suddenly, Hank circled her wrist, his fingers warm and tight. "What are you looking at?"

Caught. "N-nothing."

"Sure about that?"

His eyes were glittering and hot—maybe he did want her?—but he dropped his hand as if she'd burned him.

She'd imagined the need in his eyes. Wishful thinking, period.

Face warm, she settled her attention on the baby carrier. "I'm going to take Drew home and let you get some sleep."

"That's a good idea."

She bent and carefully positioned the still-slumbering infant into the carrier, snapping the leg holes shut around his little thighs. As she lifted the contraption, Hank helped her slip the straps over her shoulders, his touch as light and impersonal as a stranger's.

And why should it be any different? Despite his

help, despite Mia's warm feelings for him, they barely knew each other.

Just when had she started lusting after him, anyway? She must need more sleep.

"It's still dark out." Hank tugged on a pair of socks, the mattress bowing under his weight. "I'll walk you home."

Mia shook her head. "You don't have to do that. It's only two hundred and fifty feet, and you need your rest."

"It's Saturday," he said as he stood and toed into a pair of sneakers. "I'll sleep in."

He grabbed a flashlight and opened the door. It was close to dawn but still dark. In the chill air Mia's breath looked like smoke. The waning half-moon shone through the trees and bathed the ground in silvery light. Tails wagging, Ginger and Nugget trotted from the doghouse. Hank opened the gate and let them out. He patted them both, then pointed the flashlight on the ground. Mia leashed Ginger then following the beam, the group headed away from the construction and across the meadow.

She walked beside Hank, neither speaking. Somewhere an owl hooted to the accompaniment of the gurgling creek. In no time they reached her cabin.

At the door, he shut off the flashlight. His face was barely visible in the night, making his expression difficult to read.

"Thank you for taking care of Drew," she said. "You have no idea how much I appreciate that."

He shrugged. "Like I said before, no problem."

In the awkward silence that sprung up between them Hank shifted his weight from one foot to the other. He touched her cheek. She knew that touch, and her body yearned for more. Lifting her face, she offered her mouth.

But he dropped his hand and moved away. "Good night, Mia. 'Night, Drew." He turned to go.

"Wait," she said, catching his arm.

He froze. "What?"

Standing on her toes, she kissed his cheek. His face was scratchy and warm. He made a strangled sound and stiffened, his rejection as clear as the moon.

Humiliated, she stepped back. "Sorry."

"Forget it," he said, but he sounded angry. "C'mon, Nugget, let's go home."

Man and dog slipped into the darkness.

SATURDAY AFTERNOON Mia held Drew and peered anxiously through the living-room window, watching for Sookie's eleven-year-old maroon car. "She'll be here soon," she told the baby, angling sideways so he could see out. "Then we'll give you a bath."

Not wanting to miss out on anything, Ginger wagged her tail and nosed the window beside them.

Rags, who didn't care what was out there, slept curled up on the armchair. With the soft, rainy mist muting the vibrant spring colors, the cat wasn't missing much.

From here, Mia could make out the chain-link fence circling Hank's construction site. When she caught herself squinting in that direction, she shifted her attention to the small buds on a forsythia bush near the window.

Last night had been a terrible mistake. Sleeping on Hank's couch, leaving him to take care of Drew. What had she been thinking?

There was the trouble. Exhausted and scared that she might accidentally hurt the baby, she hadn't thought beyond the need to keep him safe. So she'd walked over uninvited. Judging by Hank's expression, she hadn't exactly been welcome. But the man had good manners, so he'd showed her the construction plans and offered her coffee. She'd taken advantage of him by overstaying and overstepping the shaky bounds between them.

Cringing, she shifted Drew in her arms. Her worst mistake had come at her own front door. What in the world had possessed her to kiss Hank? Yes, it was an innocent thank-you-for-everything kiss on the cheek. But he had rejected it all the same—rejected her. Heat prickled her face, and she felt the humiliation all over again.

Besides, she was lying to herself. Her motives hadn't been so innocent. She'd wanted Hank to pull her close and capture her mouth in a searing kiss. In all honesty she'd longed for more than kisses, which confused her no end. She truly didn't want a man in her life, didn't have the time. And anyway, with Drew strapped to her chest, a passionate anything would have been impossible. No, she hadn't been thinking at all.

Two blackbirds cawed and flew past the window on their way to the madronas. Ginger woofed softly. The birds caught Drew's attention, too. He made a funny little sound and wrinkled his cute baby nose.

"Those are blackbirds," she told him. "They're noisy and smart, and will eat anything."

The baby looked alert. He seemed interested. Or maybe he knew her voice. After nearly a week of her babble, he should. His eyes fixed on her face. Mia's heart swelled to bursting with warmth and tenderness. She couldn't help smiling.

"I suppose I shouldn't have bothered Sookie on her day off," she went on. Her friend had bathed Drew every day so far. Mia gladly would have let her do it forever. But she'd insisted that Mia take over the chore, starting today. So there was no reason for her to stop by.

But Bart coached a peewee field hockey team, which kept him busy most Saturdays in the spring and summer. Sookie attended the games but not the practice sessions. Today was a practice day, and when Mia had called and invited her friend over, she'd eagerly accepted. Since Mia didn't trust herself or feel comfortable alone with Drew, she was relieved and more than grateful.

"I'm twenty-nine years old and a seasoned veterinarian. I should be able to bathe a baby by myself," she told the boy and her pets. "But the truth is, I'm nervous."

The wind gusted, whipping the light rain into a downpour, as if Mother Nature herself were uneasy. Mia shuddered at the notion. Immediately, Drew stiffened.

Fast, furious drops pelted the window. "Hear that?" she asked in an attempt to soothe him. "That's the sound of the rain."

He shifted restlessly in her arms. He tried to chew his fist, but didn't seem to know how to capture it. His little forehead furrowed and his mouth screwed into a frown.

Dear God, he was going to cry.

"What's wrong, Drew?" she asked, wishing he could tell her. "You can't be hungry, because you finished a full bottle less than an hour ago. And I just changed your diaper."

Maybe he needed to burp. She placed him over her shoulder and patted his back the way Hank did.

Instead of burping, he flailed his little arms, pumped his legs and issued increasingly unhappy noises.

Mia jiggled him, but that seemed to make things worse. What should she do? Hank would know what to do, but after last night, she wouldn't bother him. *Drew can feel your tension,* he'd said. She'd best calm down.

She pulled in a breath and tried to relax. The baby wailed loud enough to wake every nocturnal animal around. So much for relaxing. Ginger raised her head and offered long, high-pitched howls. Rags jumped from the sofa and darted behind it.

"Please don't cry," Mia pleaded.

Panicked, she again patted the baby's back. Surely he'd stop crying soon, she assured herself as she paced a loop through the living room, into the kitchen and back.

But the cries escalated into screams. Her panic grew until she was as stiff and tense as the telephone wires strung outside. *Please don't die, please don't die, please don't die.*

Ginger, too, was afraid. Hanging her head, she limped to her mattress in the kitchen, lay down and hid her face under her paw.

When Mia saw Sookie's car pull up the dirt drive a few minutes later, she hurried into the kitchen and flung open the back door.

Ginger and Rags shot out, nearly knocking her

over. "Come back," she called as she righted herself. With Drew flailing away and the rain pounding down, she couldn't chase after them.

"Help," she entreated as her friend flipped the hood of her raincoat over her head and exited the car.

Sookie nodded. "Here, Ginger."

She snagged the dog in a hug, then shepherded her toward the house. Rags raced toward the meadow. He'd always been an outdoor cat, so Mia didn't worry. Once Drew settled down and the noise stopped, he'd be back.

The moment the thought entered her mind, the baby's screams ramped up a notch. Make that, *if* Drew settled down.

At the door a slightly winded, dripping Sookie wiped her feet on the mat. Ginger shook herself and, looking guilty, slunk away. In one smooth move, Sookie shrugged out of her raincoat and closed the door. She hung up her slicker on the coatrack, then aimed a worried look from Drew to Mia.

"You said the soy formula was working."

"I thought it was," Mia yelled over the noise. "He started crying about ten minutes ago and I can't get him to stop." Frustrated and scared, she threw her friend a helpless look. "What's wrong with him, Sookie?"

"I'm sure he's fine. Aren't you, little Drew?" Her friend took the screaming baby. "There, there," she soothed, gently rocking him. "Aunt Sookie's here."

For a moment nothing changed. Then to Mia's relief, the baby stopped crying. Heaving tiny, shuddering breaths, he began to settle down.

"Thank goodness," she breathed. "How did you do that?"

"I don't know. Maybe I'm not as nervous with him?"

That, or Drew was smart enough to realize what a rotten caretaker Mia was. Further proof that she should give him up. Discouraged, she threw up her hands and turned away. *Why did you entrust your son to me, Rosanne?*

"Hey you're a fast learner. You'll get the hang of this baby stuff in no time. You want to hold Drew now?"

"No." Mia crossed her arms against her chest. "He'll just cry. You keep him."

"Okay." Sookie cuddled the baby. She glanced at Mia. "I've gotta say, despite Drew's crying jag, you look a lot more rested than yesterday."

"I slept ten hours last night, thanks to Hank."

"What?" Her friend's eyes widened. "How does he fit in with your getting a good night's sleep?"

"It's a long story. Let's just say, he helped me when I needed him."

"I don't care if it's an epic tale, you can't leave me in suspense." Sookie leaned forward and arched her eyebrows. "Did he spend the night?"

"No, I was at his place. I fell asleep on his couch." Mia sent her a pointed look. "End of story."

"Back up," Sookie said. Using her foot, she pulled a kitchen chair from the table. She sat, settling Drew on her lap. "What were you doing on Hank's couch? Making out, maybe?"

"Don't you ever quit?" Raising her gaze to the yellow ceiling, Mia shook her head. "I stopped by to tell him he was right about Drew and colic. He went to make coffee. That's when I fell asleep."

"What a waste of opportunity," Sookie quipped. "I guess you don't hate the man, after all."

Hardly. "I never said I did, Sookie. I just don't like the noise and destruction of the woods."

"Did he show you the model of the house?"

Mia nodded. "It's beautiful. And he's working hard to preserve as much of the habitat as possible, and trying to replant what he can."

"By the dreamy expression on your face, I'd say you like Hank Adams." She scrutinized Mia a moment, then grinned. "A whole lot."

Mia's face warmed, but there was no sense lying to her best friend. She nodded. "Too bad it's totally one-sided."

"But you're so wonderful and so pretty. How could it possibly be one-sided?"

Her friend was biased. Mia knew she was no dazzling beauty. And she had no desire to analyze why Hank wasn't attracted to her. "It is what it is," she said.

She glanced at Drew, who stared at her through big blue eyes. He was awfully still. "Why is he so quiet?" Funny how she worried whether he was crying or not. If she hadn't been so scared she would have laughed at herself. Instead she peered anxiously at him. "Do you think something's wrong?"

"Relax, hon. After that cry, he's probably worn out. How about we give him that bath now, before he falls asleep? You fill the sink and I'll get him ready."

Sookie laid the baby on a towel spread on the old tile counter. While she undressed Drew, Mia scoured and rinsed out the kitchen sink. She fit the stopper into the drain, then placed a second clean, folded face towel over it. She turned on the tap, testing the water to make sure it was the right temperature.

"Baby's ready," Sookie said.

"Do you want to bathe him?" Mia asked hopefully.

Her friend shook her head. "I'm just here for moral support." She handed Drew to Mia. "He's all yours."

Nervous but determined, supporting his head and his soft, round bottom, Mia lowered him into the water. "Here goes," she muttered, bracing for another round of crying.

Drew stiffened. His forehead furrowed and his mouth turned down at the corners. She sucked in an apprehensive breath. "Please don't cry again."

His gaze fastened on hers. He flailed his arms and kicked his little legs. Instead of crying, he looked around.

"That's a happy boy," Sookie noted.

Judging by the pleased look on his little face, she was right. Drew seemed to like the splashes made by his own movements, and repeated them several times.

He was so cute. Warmth filled Mia's heart. She couldn't stop a fond smile. "This isn't so bad."

"Of course not. Can you handle the rest of the bath while I heat up the water and fill the tea balls?"

"I think we've earned a cup of tea," Mia said.

A few minutes later Sookie held out a towel. Mia wrapped up Drew, then carried him to the guest bedroom where she'd put the crib, dresser and changing table inherited from Rosanne. Proud that she'd managed the bath without a single tear, she hummed as she diapered and dressed him. All smiles, she carried him back to the kitchen.

"Tah-dah," she said, showing him to Sookie.

"The little guy cleans up nice." Her mouth quirked as she regarded Mia. "But you're a mess."

Mia glanced at her soaked sweatshirt and jeans, surprised that she was wet. She'd been too focused on the baby to notice. For some reason, that tickled her, and for the first time in over a week, she laughed. "Guess I'd better change."

Looking unimpressed, Drew yawned. "Nap time," Mia said. "I'll put him down, slip into dry clothes and be right back."

As she reached the hallway that led to the bedrooms, the phone rang.

"I'll get that," Sookie called.

"Thanks. If it's someone with a sick animal, tell them to come on over."

Mia settled Drew in his crib. Then she exchanged her soaked jeans and shirt for dry ones. Ready to sit down and talk to Sookie until the patient showed up or Drew awoke, she headed for the kitchen.

Sookie's solemn expression put her on alert. Mia frowned. "Who called, and what's wrong?"

"A Susan Pearson from the adoption agency. She wants you to call back right away."

Chapter Six

The adoption agency had called. Mia heard the news without absorbing it. "Already?" She sank into a chair. "It's only been five days since I met with the attorney. I didn't expect to hear so soon. Especially on a weekend."

"Some people work Saturdays," Sookie said.

"I guess so."

Mia felt her friend's scrutiny but she couldn't look at her, not right now. She plopped a tea ball, stuffed with peppermint leaves, into her mug of hot water. The agency must have found a family for Drew. That was what she wanted—wasn't it?—and she should be relieved.

Peppermint was supposed to soothe the nerves, so she leaned over the steam and inhaled the scented fumes. Didn't do much for the heart, though. She felt as if someone had kicked her there.

"Mrs. Pearson asked that you call right back,"

Sookie prodded. She gestured to the pink pad tacked to the wall near the phone. "She left her *home* number."

"She'll just have to wait. Right now, I want to talk about you. What's going on—"

"We'll get to me in a minute," Sookie interrupted. Nibbling her thumbnail thoughtfully, she aimed an assessing look at Mia. "You're upset about this. Are you sure you want to give up Drew?"

"What do you mean, am I sure I want to give him up?" Mia repeated, stalling for time.

Did she?

Yes, her rational mind assured her. Allowing others to care for and raise Drew was the best way to keep him safe.

Her heart wasn't so certain. She pulled the tea ball from her mug and set it aside. "I don't have much choice."

Sookie rolled her eyes. "Come on, Mia, this is the twenty-first century. Plenty of women raise kids alone, and do a darn good job of it."

She'd misinterpreted the reason for Mia's hesitation. Single parenthood wasn't the problem. What could happen to Drew in her care was what frightened her. She shuddered at the thought.

"Your gran did a bang-up job with you, didn't she?" Sookie asked.

The woman had raised Mia with love and guidance, had taught her to enjoy and respect the woods and the animals who lived here. She nodded. "Gran was the best."

If she were here now, Mia knew she'd agree with the decision to let a deserving couple adopt Drew. Given what had happened, it was the right choice.

Sookie didn't know about Gracie. She never would. Mia had locked the tragic event deep inside herself, where it would stay.

"You wouldn't be alone," Sookie continued. "Aunt Sookie will always be here to lend a hand. Everybody around here adores you, Mia, and I don't know one person who won't come running if you need them. All those people to love Drew and help you."

The kind words warmed Mia's heart, but didn't change anything. "I appreciate that, Sookie, but I can't adopt Drew. And if you don't mind, I don't want to discuss it anymore." She folded her hands on the table and leaned forward. "Now, what's going on with you and Bart?"

Her friend tilted her head and batted her lashes in mock naiveté. "Whatever are you talking about?"

"That Mona Lisa smile leads me to believe you have a juicy secret." Mia hoped so. She needed a diversion.

"I do." Sookie, too, leaned forward. "Promise you won't breathe a word of this."

Mia made an X over her heart.

"It all started when you brought Drew home. He's so precious." Sookie's face softened longingly. "Watching Drew and helping you take care of him made me realize how badly I want a baby of my own."

That sounded reasonable. Mia nodded. "And?"

"I wasn't sure whether Bart was ready. I figured the best time to discuss the matter was the night of our anniversary. Remember how excited I was?"

Mia nodded. "You bought that sexy black teddy on your lunch break."

"To seduce him into wanting a baby."

"Ah. Well, did it work?"

Sookie winked. "He loved the outfit, but I only wore it five minutes." She smiled widely. "Interestingly enough Bart's been thinking about kids, too. That very night we worked on making a baby. We've been working on it every chance we get." Mia envied the twinkle in her friend's eye. "Hopefully we'll be pregnant in the near future." She lifted her mug. "Will you toast to that?"

Mia clinked rims with her friend. "Here's to good news for you and Bart."

"And here's to your getting Hank's attention."

"That's not going to happen," Mia said. But she clinked rims again, just in case.

YAWNING, Hank rolled his cart down the aisle of the near-empty Dobson's General Store, where he had come to pick up dog food and the week's groceries. One of the wheels squeaked whenever he turned a corner, but the pop music playing over the P.A. system almost drowned out the obnoxious sound. Fluorescent lights brightened the windowless wood building, but didn't prevent it from looking dingy.

Most people stayed home Sunday mornings or went to church, which was why he was here now, when he wasn't likely to have to deal with long lines. Though, with Forest Glen's scant population, the store wasn't ever really crowded.

He headed for the frozen food section, wincing with every step. He'd pushed himself hard yesterday, ordering windows and lining up supplies for next week's schedule, and when the rain let up midafternoon, working on the framing till dark. Today he was paying for it with sore muscles that demanded a break.

Too bad he couldn't shut off his mind, which was full of Mia and Drew. Had the baby slept well, giving Mia a chance to rest? Why did she want to give him up, when it was obvious she loved him? What had happened to scare her so much?

Wanting to know meant he was starting to care. Hank didn't want to care.

He berated himself for giving in to kissing her while she'd slept.

Then she'd kissed him. Though she'd barely

grazed his cheek, he'd felt the soft press of her lips clear to his soul. The woman had awakened the physical hunger he'd tamped down for so long. Now he wanted her day and night. That scared him witless.

Worse, she seemed to be attracted to him.

If she saw his mangled body, her desire would quickly turn into disgust. Grimacing at the thought, Hank opened the freezer door. He wouldn't touch her again, and wouldn't let her touch him.

He tossed several frozen dinners, two pizzas with all the toppings and a quart of blueberry ice cream into the cart. What else did he need? Milk, cereal, bread, lunch meat, cheese and a couple of apples. Junk food, pop, dog food and a treat for Nugget. He repeated the list over and over like a mantra as he headed for the dairy section one aisle over. Anything to keep his mind off Mia.

Suddenly there she was. In the deli section. Naturally, Drew was with her, his car seat filling most of her cart. Dread settled like wet concrete in Hank's gut while, at the same time, his heart gave a joyous little leap. Rubbing his chest, he frowned.

She was reaching for a package of cheese and didn't see him. He could back away and leave and she'd never know. He shook his head. That wasn't his style. He was an adult; he'd deal with this— make some small-talk comment—and move on.

When he wheeled forward, the squeak caught her attention.

Her eyes widened and the familiar flush stained her cheeks. "Hello."

He nodded soberly. "Morning."

He couldn't help noting the shadows in and under her eyes. Either Drew still kept her up or something else weighed on her. He glanced at the tiny boy, sleeping soundly and looking healthy. "How's the kid today?"

Mia followed his gaze to the baby. "Doing better, thanks. He woke up three times last night, but went right back to sleep after he ate."

Though the store was warm, she rubbed her arms as if she were cold.

"When he wakes up, tell him I said, 'Good job, squirt.'"

Her mouth quirked up at the corners, hinting at a smile. Then her lips straightened. Any minute now she'd start chewing the lower one.

Hank told himself he didn't want to know what was bothering her. He grabbed the handle of his cart, intending to say his goodbye and head off. "So what's wrong?" he heard himself ask.

"Actually, I have good news," she said, her solemn face at odds with her words. "Yesterday I heard from the adoption agency. They've lined up several prospective families for Drew. The paperwork will be here early next week."

"What does that mean, paperwork?"

"The information about each family. Where they live, whether they have other kids, their occupations, stuff like that. I'm supposed to read through it and choose one. Then I'll meet the couple in person, and see how they interact with Drew."

Hank nodded. "Sounds fair enough. And it's what you want." Or so she claimed.

"Yeah." She didn't seem happy about it.

"Hey, you don't have to choose any of them."

"If they're not the right family for Drew, I won't," she said, jutting up her chin as if defending the baby.

In the silence that fell between them, he shuffled his feet. He'd said hello, now it was time to go. He shoved his hands into his back pockets. "See you around."

"Why don't you come over for dinner tonight?" She looked as surprised by the invitation as he was. "As a way to thank you for helping me with Drew the other night." Expression hopeful, she leaned toward him.

His heart gave a pleased kick. He ignored it. "I said I didn't mind. You don't owe me anything."

For a second, confusion colored her expression. Then her face closed. She gave a brisk nod. "Oh. I see. You don't want to come."

"Trust me, Mia, it's not you."

The hell it wasn't. He wanted her. That was dangerous and impossible and stupid, to boot.

"No problem, really." She offered a thin smile, then bent toward the sleeping baby and fussed with his blanket. "I'd better finish shopping before Drew wakes up. Be sure to pat Nugget for me."

She turned to go. The lonely evening loomed ahead, all the emptier after seeing her. He couldn't face that. Cursing himself for a fool, he reached out to pull her back. Changed his mind about touching her—that was risky—and cleared his throat instead.

"I'd like to come for dinner. What time should I show up, and what should I bring?"

As she pivoted toward him, her face brightened. "Come at six, and bring Nugget."

HOURS LATER, with Drew, Ginger and Rags to keep her company and a savory pot of beef stew simmering on the stove, Mia hummed as she diced a green pepper for the salad. Glancing up, she smiled at the baby propped on the kitchen table in his baby carrier.

"Hank's coming to dinner, Drew."

The boy gurgled as if he recognized his own name. Or maybe he approved of their dinner guest. For the moment he seemed content—a good omen of the night to come?

For no reason at all, Mia laughed. She felt flushed

and happy, like a silly high school girl with a crush on someone who had finally noticed her.

Which was ridiculous. She was a woman, not a girl. And Hank wasn't attracted to her. She really shouldn't make this more than what it was—a dinner between neighbors. The best thing about tonight was that her focus on making a nice meal kept her from stressing over the papers soon to arrive from the adoption agency. She dreaded reading through the documents and selecting the best family for Drew. What if she made the wrong choice? She wasn't looking forward to the face-to-face interview that would follow, either. Or handing Drew to his new parents and walking away.

Her heart seemed to clench in her chest. *Don't think about that now.*

She forced her attention back to where it had been a few moments ago. On making dinner. The stew smelled heavenly. She dipped a spoon into the sim-mering pot and scooped up meat, potatoes, sauce and vegetables, which she emptied onto a saucer. After the spoonful cooled a bit, she sampled it.

"Not bad," she told Ginger and Rags, who both aimed pleading looks at her. "But I need second opinions." She fed each a chunk of meat.

Dog and cat barely chewed before licking their mouths with satisfaction. "What do you think?" she asked. "Does it need salt?"

Neither animal seemed to think so, and she agreed. She left the remaining stew alone.

"Now to whip up a batch of Gran's famous biscuits," she said. "Then I'll set the table. Last, I'll change my clothes and make myself presentable."

The secret biscuit recipe had been handed down to her with instructions to keep it within the family. Mia had respected Gran's wishes. She was the only person who knew the ingredients. The knowledge probably would die with her.

A sad thought, but she had no one to share it with—except Drew. But she likely wouldn't see him again once he was adopted. That dampened her spirits considerably.

As if Drew could read her mind, he made a distressed sound. "Believe me, a new family is the best thing for you," she told him.

True, but Dear God, that hurt.

Ten minutes before six, just as she popped the biscuits into the oven, Drew started to fuss. He cried while she changed him and kept at it while she mixed a bottle and warmed it. His frantic screaming didn't stop until she shoved the nipple into his mouth. Suckling hungrily, he quickly polished off the entire bottle.

As she burped him, she heard the front door buzzer. *Hank.* Her gaze darted to the clock. Oh, no, it was after six. She wasn't ready! Her jeans were dirty from where she'd wiped her doughy hands. Splotches of spit-up streaked her blouse. She hadn't combed her hair, applied lipstick or dabbed perfume behind her ears. Too late now.

With Drew propped over her shoulder and the animals at her heels, she hurried to the living room. On the way to the door she peeked through the window. Hank was clutching a bouquet of flowers and was dressed in a tan corduroy sports jacket, chocolate-brown turtleneck and jeans. He looked handsome enough to eat.

She, however, looked like a total slob. Forcing a smile, she opened the door. "Please come in."

Tail wagging, Nugget yipped and raced for Ginger. The dogs jumped playfully at each other, which sent Rags diving under the couch.

"Am I early?"

She let out a sigh. "No, I'm late."

"These are for you." He held out a bouquet of tulips, daisies, tiger lilies and forsythia. Then, seeming to realize her hands were full with Drew, pulled them to his chest.

"Thank you, Hank," Mia said. "They're beautiful. Did you pick them yourself?"

Ears turning red, he nodded. "I didn't like the prepackaged stuff at Dobson's so I went for a walk. Where can I find a vase?"

"In the kitchen. I'll show you."

He sniffed the air. "Is something burning?"

Mia smelled it, too. "My biscuits!"

She pushed Drew into Hank's arms, then dashed into the kitchen.

The room was hazy with smoke. Coughing, she slid the charred biscuits from the oven and dropped the pan into the sink. Nose wrinkled, she opened the back door. Cool evening air rushed in, dispelling the smoke. When Hank and Drew followed a moment later, she was scraping the burned mess into the garbage.

"Guess we're not having bread tonight," she said.

Hank shrugged. "We'll live."

Her gaze settled on the bouquet. The pretty flowers he'd carefully picked were smashed and broken. She threw him a sheepish look. "I did that when I handed over Drew, huh?"

"No worries." He glanced down at the boy in the crook of one arm. Then, mouth quirked, he shook his head at the flowers. "Some of them are okay."

It was a good thing this wasn't intended as a romantic dinner. Mia filled her Gran's favorite green-glass vase with water and arranged the flowers as best she could, then set the vase in the center of the table.

"There. It's still lovely." She caught a whiff of stale milk, glanced down at her blouse, and offered an apologetic smile. "I ought to change my clothes."

"Don't do it on my account," Hank said. "You look fine."

Given that he wasn't attracted to her, of course her appearance didn't make a difference to him. From his place in the crook of Hank's arm Drew yawned and his eyelids drooped.

"Looks as if the little squirt's ready for a nap. Perfect timing," Hank quipped.

"I'll put him to bed. Let's hope he sleeps through dinner."

HANK SCRAPED the last of the stew from his bowl. Mia had cooked a great meal, the best food he'd eaten in months. "That was delicious."

"I'm glad you liked it." She nudged the half-empty tureen of stew toward him. "Would you like a glass of wine? I could open a bottle."

"I don't drink," he said, earning a curious look. "But I will help myself to seconds."

She watched him fill his own bowl, then held out hers. "May I have more, too?"

"Sure thing."

Hank liked that she ate heartily, unlike some women. He liked her warm smile and relaxed manner, too. Truth was, he liked everything about her.

"Too bad about the biscuits," she said. "They're especially good with stew. Great for sopping up the last drop."

"I'll have to come back for them some other time," he said without thinking.

She smiled and swallowed a mouthful before she replied. "It's a deal. But you may have to watch Drew so they don't burn."

"For another meal like this, I'd be glad to." And he meant that.

Hank was shocked by how comfortable this felt—sharing a meal with Mia as though they were good friends. Yet they barely knew each other.

"So," she said as she set down her spoon, "how long have you been in construction?"

"Years. I got my first construction job the summer before I started college, and worked every vacation and every summer in the field." He laid his spoon in his empty bowl. "I liked it so much, I earned a degree in civil engineering. I've been building houses ever since."

"Impressive," Mia commented, looking at him with respect.

"But you treat and save animals' lives. That's much more important." Hank gestured toward the dogs and cat. "Just ask them."

She dipped her head in modest acknowledgment. "Thank you."

"I had a dog when I was a kid, just a mutt my dad brought home from the pound." Hank shook his head, remembering. "Can you believe I named him

Spot?" He grinned. "Not very original, but I sure did love that animal. If he hadn't had such a good vet, old Spot never would have lived fourteen years."

"That's a long time for a dog," Mia said.

She'd propped her hand on her chin and seemed to want to hear more, so he went on.

"Spot and I used to explore, mostly places where we weren't supposed to go. He cut himself and got slivers in his paws. Once he got stuck in a hole. My dad had to dig him out. Poor Spot had ripped up his shoulder something awful."

"That's terrible," Mia said sympathetically.

Hank nodded. "I know, I know. I felt real bad about that, and vowed to behave myself and stay in the neighborhood from that day on."

"And did you?"

"Tried. Spot wanted no part of that. He was an adventurer, and I followed him into it." He shrugged. "What was I supposed to do, miss out on all the fun?"

She laughed, a pretty sound that teased a chuckle from Hank. "I'll bet your mother had her hands full with both of you."

She had that right. His mother claimed he'd given her a head full of gray hair. His grin was unrepentant. "She says I was worse than my brother and sister combined."

"Tell me about them, and your parents."

"My folks have been married forty years. Dad ran a printing business, and Mom helped out. Now they're retired. My brother, Jake, is the oldest. He's divorced. I'm next, and Lisa's the baby of the family. She's married to Ryan, and they have two kids. That's how I know about babies and colic." He didn't want to say more, so he shrugged.

Mia nodded. "Any other relatives?"

"Let's see." Hank rubbed his chin. "Three aunts, two uncles, one grandma and a bunch of cousins."

"Wow," she said with wonder. "So many. I envy you."

"It's a crowd, all right."

"Do you miss them while you're here?"

"I do," he said, surprised at the truth of the statement. It had been months since he'd spoken to any of them. A long time, but since Gil's death, they were way too careful around him. Then when Kristin had walked out, their sympathy had turned into a smothering pity he didn't want or need. Still, he ought to call and check in.

Mia studied him thoughtfully, looking as if she wanted to pry deeper into his life. Sooner or later the ugly part of his past would surface—how he had contributed to the death of his best friend, and the sorry mess he'd made of his life. That'd wipe out her respect for him.

He didn't think he could handle that. He pushed

aside his dishes and shifted forward, resting his forearms on the table. "What about you?" he asked, wanting to know more about her. "I know you moved to Forest Glen when you were five. Where were you before that?"

Her face darkened as if clouds suddenly appeared overhead. "I was born in Olympia, Washington." She toyed with her water glass, her eyes fixed on the diamond pattern etched into the glass. "I lived there until I moved here to live with my granny."

He knew her family were all gone, but he didn't know the details. His turn to pry. "What happened, if you don't mind my asking."

For a minute he didn't think she'd answer. Frowning at a water ring left by the glass, she blotted it with her napkin. At last she sighed and raised her gaze. "My father left home when I was five and a half. A month later, my mother dropped me off here. I never saw either of them again," she stated matter-of-factly while she crumpled the napkin. "They've both been dead several years now."

Hank imagined Mia as a little kid, losing her father and then her mother. That kind of rejection had to hurt. Compared to hers, his childhood had been paradise.

He wanted to comfort her, but didn't know how. He settled on simple words. "I'm sorry."

"It was a long time ago." She glanced at her lap. "And, anyway, it was my fault," she blurted.

Certain he'd misheard, Hank narrowed his eyes. "What?"

"Actually, I really don't want to talk about this." She slid her chair back, then nested their bowls atop the empty salad plates. "I didn't make anything for dessert, but I did buy a pint of butterscotch swirl ice cream and some caramel sauce. Would you like a sundae?"

He wanted to know more. But he had no business pushing her and no business getting involved. And he didn't want to destroy the easy mood between them. He forced a casual nod. "Sounds great."

Half an hour later, full to bursting, he groaned. "I haven't eaten this much in a long time. My poor, aching belly."

Mia's mouth quirked in humor. "You can work it off by helping me with the dishes. Would you rather wash or dry?"

He took the invitation as a sign that she still felt comfortable despite his questions. "Wash," he said. "That way you won't have to tell me where to put everything."

Mia handed him a bib apron that proclaimed I Heart Forest Glen, Washington. She donned its twin. They worked in companionable silence.

A warmth filled him. He felt good with Mia, better than he ever had with Kristin. The realization killed his contentment. He needed to leave. Now, before he got too comfortable.

Yet when Mia folded and hung up the dish towel, all he wanted was to pull her close and bury himself in her softness. By the look in her eyes, she wanted him to do just that.

A man could lose himself in those big blue eyes. "Mia," he said.

"Yes, Hank?"

She'd moved closer. He could see the silver flecks in her eyes and the tiny mole on her cheek. Her head tilted a fraction and her lips opened. His gaze dropped to her mouth, primed for his kiss.

His hands ached to hold her and his body strained toward her like a plant hungry for the sun. He could lean down and... *Do it*, his senses commanded. But one kiss would lead to another, and then they'd both want more. Until she saw his scars. Then she'd recoil in horror. He couldn't handle that.

He moved his gaze to her shoulder. "Your apron strap is twisted." He wiped his hands on the bib of his own apron, drying them. Careful not to touch her shoulder, he untwisted the strap with hands that shook.

"Thank you." The welcoming light in her eyes faded to confusion, then hurt. "We're just about through here. If you want to leave, I'll finish up by myself."

He nodded. "Tomorrow's a busy day, and I should turn in early." He clucked his tongue and Nugget jumped up, Ginger beside him.

Hank retrieved his jacket from the coatrack. Mia and the dogs walked him to the front door.

"Thanks for a great dinner," he said.

"You're welcome. I'm glad you came."

She favored him with a sweet, hungry look. The need to kiss her was strong, and he almost surrendered to it.

Flushing, Mia looked down at Ginger, releasing him from her magnetic gaze and saving him from making a big mistake.

She hooked a hand through the dog's collar. "It's safe to open the door now. Good night, Hank."

"'Night." He opened the door and walked through it.

Nugget at his side, he turned away from Mia, from the light. The door closed quietly behind him.

In the chill darkness of the night he strode home.

Chapter Seven

Tuesday afternoon, eleven-year-old, freckle-faced Avery Rogers cast a stricken look at his black-and-white rabbit. "What's wrong with Petie?"

Mia offered a reassuring smile. "It's nothing serious, Avery. Petie has ear mites."

June, the boy's plump, thirtysomething mother, a woman Mia had known for years, looked offended. "But I keep a clean house."

"I know you do, June, and your housekeeping skills have nothing to do with Petie's problem. Ear mites are common in rabbits. I'll ask Sookie to bring in a tube of antifungal cream. If you follow the instructions and apply it twice a day, Petie will be fine in no time." She glanced into Avery's anxious face. "Can you do that?"

He nodded. "Thank you, Dr. Mia."

"No problem. While you put Petie back in his cage, I'll let Sookie know what you need. I'll be right back."

She found her assistant, phone between her ear and shoulder, scribbling in the appointment book. All day long pet owners, some who had never used Mia's veterinary services, had been scheduling appointments or dropping in for shots or injuries or a quick checkup.

When Sookie hung up, Mia handed her the prescription for Petie. "Doesn't it seem busy for a Tuesday?"

Sookie nodded. "It was this way yesterday, too."

"Where are they all coming from?"

"Not to downplay your wonderful vet skills, but isn't it obvious? They all want to meet Drew."

That was probably true. Despite the sparse population and isolated houses, everybody knew about the baby. They also knew that his stay here was temporary.

The thought filled Mia with emptiness, but her mind was made up. The boy would be better off with someone else.

"Oh, the mail came." Sookie nodded her chin at the thick white envelope. "That's from the adoption agency."

The files had arrived. Mia had expected them, but she hadn't expected her heart to wrench or her stomach to twist. She couldn't deal with that, not right now. "Thanks, Sookie. I'll look at them later."

When she returned to the exam room, June looked

slightly flustered. "I wonder..." She cleared her throat. "Could Avery and I see the baby?"

Mia would have preferred to keep Drew and her personal life to herself, but in Forest Glen that wasn't easy. Before she could reply, Sookie walked in.

"Here's that cream for Petie." She looked from Mia to Avery to June, then lifted her eyebrows. "What's up?"

"Mia might show us the baby," Avery said.

He was fairly jumping with excitement and June wore an expectant look Mia couldn't ignore.

"All right." Slipping her hand into the pocket of her lab coat she fingered the portable baby monitor she used whenever Drew was in his crib. "He's asleep, but if you're quiet..."

Finger to her lips, she led the mother and boy up the clinic hall, then through the living room. Another hall led to the guest bedroom and Drew. He lay on his back, eyes closed and rosebud mouth slack in sleep. Mia's heart swelled with tenderness. She stood back while June and Avery beamed at Drew.

The woman slung her arm around her son's narrow shoulders and hugged him. Anyone could see she was a good, loving mother. A decades-old ache churned inside Mia. She could hardly remember her mother and had no recollection of what her touch felt like. Avery was a very lucky boy.

He grinned fondly at his mother, and Mia knew

she was equally lucky to have Avery. Mia could never be a mother to Drew or anyone. She'd known that for twenty-four years. Why did it hurt so much now?

They tiptoed out. "He sure is cute," June said as they returned to the examining room.

Sookie grinned from where she'd been waiting with the rabbit. "Isn't he?"

Avery nodded. "He's little, too. How old is he?"

"A little over five weeks," Mia said.

"Oh." Brow furrowed, he looked at Mia. "Why don't you want to keep him?"

"Avery!" June gasped. "That's a rude question." But her eyes gleamed with curiosity. So did Sookie's.

Mia ignored both women. "It's okay," she assured the boy, who hung his head.

How to explain in a way that made sense, without revealing the truth? "Well, I never planned on having kids. Besides, I want Drew to have two loving parents to keep him happy and safe. Like you have with your mom and dad. Does that make sense?"

The boy shrugged. "I guess."

Just then the bell on the front door tinkled.

"That's your three-thirty," Sookie said, rescuing her from June's scrutiny.

Mia heaved a sigh of relief as she waved goodbye to June, Avery and Petie.

EARLY FRIDAY MORNING, exhausted from balancing a full load of vet patients with caring for Drew, Mia lay in bed and frowned at the disgustingly bright face of the bedside clock. It was 4:00 a.m., for goodness' sake. Drew had eaten half an hour ago. At the moment the baby monitor was quiet, meaning he was asleep. He'd probably stay that way for at least a few hours. If she were smart she'd do the same. She flipped onto her back, closed her eyes and willed herself to sleep.

An instant later her eyelids popped open. No way could she relax enough to sleep. There was too much to worry about.

Drew's health, for one. Sure, at the moment he seemed fine. But that was no guarantee of anything.

Then there was his adoption. It had been three days and she had yet to read through the files Mrs. Pearson had sent. She'd been too busy.

Not too busy to leaf through a magazine last night before bed. Or to fantasize about Hank. The mere thought of the man caused her heart to flutter. She released a sigh. She'd had fun Sunday night and knew he had, too. She'd enjoyed the sound of his laughter, the stories about his childhood dog and hearing about his family.

Mia liked him. She wanted a physical relationship, even if it ended when he left Forest Glen. While

Hank wanted… What did he want? He certainly hadn't called or stopped by. Friendship? Maybe. But nothing more.

Although…over dinner, she'd caught him looking at her more than once, the warm gleam in his eyes signaling sexual interest. Or so she'd thought. Since he hadn't kissed her, though, she must have misunderstood.

Lord knew she'd given him plenty of chances over the past week. The first time the other night when she'd kissed his cheek. The second time as they stood side by side at the sink, taking care of the dishes. Hank had leaned down, his expression intent and focused with what she'd taken for interest. She'd felt sure he was going to kiss her.

Her mouth twisted as she remembered. Instead he'd straightened the strap of her apron. Then at the door just before he left, she'd raised her head and offered him another chance. She recalled the unreadable darkness in his eyes.

No, he just wasn't interested.

Still, she enjoyed his company. Having his friendship was better than nothing.

But here she was, thinking about Hank when she should be sleeping. Or reading those files. Her stomach knotted.

Finding a family to love Drew was the best way to keep him safe. Mia knew that.

Then why hadn't she opened those files? Through the darkness of the room, she glanced toward the dresser where she'd stacked them.

Mrs. Pearson and the potential families were waiting for her decision. Mia's head began to pound with the pressure to read the files right away. "It's too darn early in the morning for this," she moaned, even as she flipped on the bedside lamp.

Since she wasn't going to fall asleep, what the heck. She'd read them now. Blinking in the sudden light, she threw back the covers, got up and padded to the dresser. She clutched the stack of files to her chest and before returning to bed, glanced at the baby monitor. Drew was awfully quiet. What if there was something wrong? Filled with trepidation, she set the files on the bed and tiptoed into the baby's room.

He was on his back, which was how she'd left him. Heart thudding, she leaned over the crib, cocked her head and listened. His chest rose and fell in the soft, regular cadence of sleep. Thank goodness. She released a breath.

Returning to the files, she sat cross-legged on the bed. Which one should she open first? Undecided, she spread all three on the bed. The agency had removed the names of the prospective families, but even if each name had been spelled out in gold, she wouldn't have a clue about the people.

Did they know how to handle a colicky baby? Did they care about the woods and all its animals, and would they raise Drew to respect both? Would they love him as he should be loved, unconditionally and without limitations?

The way I love him?

And there it was. The reason for her hesitation. She loved Drew, screams, tears, spit-up, poopy diapers and all. But at any moment something might go wrong. She couldn't take that chance.

"I will read these files and decide," she ordered herself.

But paperwork seemed a cold way to choose Drew's parents, even if it was merely a precursor to a face-to-face interview. She couldn't do it. Not now. Maybe after a cup of tea.

Slipping the baby monitor into her robe pocket, she headed to the kitchen.

Ginger, who clearly had one ear cocked toward Mia's footsteps, rose awkwardly from her mattress. At eight years old she was often stiff after a long rest. But her enthusiasm flagged high as ever, and her rapidly wagging tail and toothy grin proved it.

She was a loyal companion and a trusted friend, and on this morning of reading through the files in search of the right parents for Drew, Mia was especially glad for the greeting. She squatted down to rub her pet's head. "Good morning, you."

She let go of Ginger to stroke Rags, who'd just strolled in as if he were in charge. "I suppose you two want your breakfast, huh? Let me put on the teakettle first."

While the water heated, she fed her pets. Then, leaving the tea to steep, she searched through the refrigerator for one of the packets of raw beef she kept stocked for the hawk. Meat in hand, she went to the clinic.

The raptor was quiet. Not wanting to startle him, Mia called a soft good morning before approaching the wire holding cage.

The young, red-tailed male screeched loudly and tried to flap his wings, but his injury and the confined space hindered him. His healthy reaction was a good sign that he'd grown no weaker. A few more days and she'd move him to the larger cage outside. Mia didn't want the bird getting used to her—that would hinder his reintroduction into the wilds. So she didn't speak again, simply shoved one hand into a thick leather glove, fed the meat into the cage through a door on top, checked to make sure he had water and then moved away. His shrill call and keen eyes followed her, but as soon she moved out of sight he quieted. In the moments following his shrieks, the otherwise empty clinic sounded eerily silent.

As she headed toward the utility room to wash

up, she heard the unmistakable *thwak! thwak! thwak!* of a hammer.

As always, Hank had started early. She knew his crew wouldn't arrive for several hours yet. They put in long hours, but he worked even longer, starting before they arrived and working till dark.

Mia smiled to herself. She still didn't like the noise. But she liked him.

Standing at the utility room sink, she glanced out the small window that overlooked the back of the house. It was still dark, but more gray than black. She could see the sky, its pale blue color signaling the coming sunrise. Hank and his crew would have good weather today.

As she dried her hands, baby noises blurted through the monitor. Drew was awake. Her alone time was over and she still hadn't looked at the files. Maybe tomorrow.

She hurried to the nursery. "Good morning, Drew," she said, leaning over his crib to smile at him. He'd kicked off his covers, and his bare little legs and undershirt-clad arms waved at her. "Are you hungry already? It's only been an hour."

He stared up at her. Then she noticed. His normally rosy little nose was pale, actually looked blue. His fingers and toes had the same bluish tint. Something was wrong, horribly wrong. Fear chilled her blood.

"Drew?"

She touched his face. His skin felt clammy. Her heart seemed to stop.

Dear God.

WAS THAT THE PHONE? From his uncomfortable perch on the second-story framing, Hank frowned. Enjoying the smell of the crisp, fresh morning, he'd left the trailer door open to air things out. Now, as the shrill ringing cut through the predawn bird calls, he wished he hadn't. The caller had better leave a message because he wasn't about to climb down to answer the phone—his hip and lower back hurt like a son of a bitch. Grimacing, he hammered a nail into a two-by-four.

The framework was nearly done, but there were a few odds and ends he wanted to finish before the crew showed up in a couple of hours. With the sun on the verge of rising, it was a good time to work.

At last the ringing stopped. Relieved, he pounded in another nail. Despite his aches and pains, he liked working outside while most people slept. It made him feel as if the great outdoors belonged to him, the birds, Nugget and any creature who happened to be awake.

The damn phone rang again. Twenty feet below, Nugget woofed from his dog run. He glanced up at Hank and whined.

What in hell? Scowling, Hank set down the hammer. He squinted at his watch. Four frickin' forty-five. Who'd phone at this hour? Somebody from the crew, calling in sick? Whoever it was, they didn't want to leave a message. Must be important, and that couldn't be good.

Worry tightened Hank's gut. "All right, all right," he told Nugget, "I'm coming down."

He hoped to God nothing had happened to one of his parents. He'd called them the other night, talking to them for the first time in months. They'd been pleased to hear from him and had seemed fine, but you never knew. He'd also called his sister and brother, but hadn't been able to reach either one. He'd left messages. But neither Lisa nor Jake would call at this hour—unless something was wrong.

The phone was still ringing as his feet hit the dirt.

"Hank Adams," he grunted into the phone, panting to catch his breath.

"It's Mia. Something's wrong with Drew. He's turning blue."

She sounded panicky. Terrified. "Calm down, Mia," he said, but the truth was, she had him scared, too. He scrubbed his hand over his face. Schooling his voice to mask his own anxiety, he asked, "Where is Drew now? Is he breathing?"

"He's right here with me, and I think so. Hold on

while I check." A beat of silence passed. "Yes, he's definitely breathing."

"That's good. Now, did you call the doctor?"

"He's not in this early," she answered, clearly upset. "His answering service took my name and said I should take Drew to the twenty-four-hour family clinic."

Hank nodded. "Sounds like a good idea."

"It's twenty miles from here. I don't think I can drive *and* look after Drew, especially with his car seat in the back. Will you come with us?"

Hank didn't even hesitate. "I'll be right there."

"Hurry."

He scribbled a quick note for his crew and tacked it to the front door. Then glanced at Nugget, nosing the chain-link fence. "Keep an eye on things, mutt. I'll be back."

Chapter Eight

Mia bit her lip as the doctor, an attractive, thirtysomething woman whose name badge identified her as Dr. Mohr, examined Drew with a practiced hand. Stripped down to his diaper, he lay on the exam table. Dr. Mohr was so gentle he didn't even cry, just gazed up at her with bright, attentive eyes.

Mia, however, was tied in knots. The baby's skin had a definite blue tinge. What was wrong with him? Was it his lungs or his heart?

Please don't die. Please.

She was so scared she could barely think. Her ice-cold hands locked over her clenched stomach and her legs shook. She wouldn't have been able to stand if not for Hank.

His solid arm rested protectively around her shoulders, offering comfort and reassurance. She wasn't too proud to soak up both. They hovered close to Drew, keeping out of the doctor's way, but staying within arm's reach. Both locked their attention on the tiny, bluish baby.

Dr. Mohr finished the exam. She tucked a blanket over Drew, then turned toward Mia and Hank, her expression open and relaxed. "There's not a thing wrong with this baby."

Mia wasn't certain she'd heard right. She slanted her head and frowned. "How can that be?"

Hank took a firmer tack. "If Drew's okay, why does he look blue?"

"Because he's cold."

"Cold?" Mia echoed.

The doctor nodded, and Drew blew bubbles. "He's a little baby. He doesn't have much fat to keep him warm."

Hank let out a breath. "So other than being cold, he's fine?"

Dr. Mohr smiled and nodded. "A healthy, normal baby."

"Thank God," Mia sighed. The relief that flooded her was so strong, she sagged against Hank. "So I should dress him in more layers and warmer clothes?"

"Not necessarily. Babies can get overheated, too. A good rule of thumb is, if the temperature is too warm for you to wear a heavy sweater comfortably, then it's too warm for him. If you're worried he's cold, check his hands and feet. If they feel cold, he's cold." She regarded Mia with a kindly expression. "Do you have any other questions or concerns?"

Mia shook her head. "Not at the moment."

Everything the doctor said made good, common sense. She was a competent veterinarian, able to diagnose animals with skill and certainty. How could she have been so stupid about this?

Just like that, the faint hope she'd carried and buried so deep she hadn't admitted it even to herself—that maybe she'd make a fit mother after all—died. She must give up Drew, right away, a clean, quick cut that would leave him with few scars. If it meant staying up all night, she'd read those adoption files and make her decision before tomorrow morning.

Wrenching pain filled her chest. She must have looked as tormented as she felt, for Dr. Mohr glanced at her with concern.

"Don't beat yourself up about this," she counseled. "You're not the first couple this has happened to, and it's better to err on the safe side. At nearly six weeks, a baby's brain isn't sufficiently developed for his internal thermostat to work properly. That's why this happened. Be assured, you and your husband haven't done your son any harm."

"He's not my s—" Mia started.

"Thanks very much," Hank interrupted. "Where do we pay?"

The doctor told him, then glanced from Hank to Mia. "We're not busy at this hour, so stay as long as you need to. Please leave the door open when you go so we'll know the room is available for the next patient." She glanced once more at Drew. "Your son is developing just fine. You're doing a good job." Offering a reassuring smile, she exited, closing the door behind her.

As Mia dressed Drew, she frowned at Hank. "Why did you let her think we're Drew's parents, or that you and I are married? I'm not your wife, and I am not Drew's mother."

"Jeez, Mia, don't you think I know that? It seemed easier than trying to explain."

"There's nothing easy about this situation."

"You're being too hard on yourself—"

"And you have no idea what you're talking about."

Drew was starting to fuss, making it difficult to fit his flailing legs into the feet of his sleeper. Hank tried to help but she elbowed him away. Hands raised in a conciliatory gesture, expression wary, he backed up until the wall stopped him.

Wasn't that just perfect? She'd pushed away the very person she needed, the man who had dropped everything this morning to help her. That made her feel even worse, but she wasn't ready to apologize. Mouth tight, she managed to pull on the sleeper and snap it closed.

Drew stiffened and started to cry, which scared her all over again. "I intend to find him a new home as soon as possible, where people know enough to keep him warm."

Hank opened his mouth but before he could speak, she cut him off. "I appreciate your help, Hank, but I don't want to discuss this."

She wrapped Drew in his baby blanket, picked him up and cuddled him. He wouldn't quiet down, nor could Mia stop her own tears. Something had broken inside her and she couldn't hold in the pain. Soberly, Hank handed her a tissue from the box on the small desk in the room.

The thoughtful gesture only made her cry more. She was exhausted and so unhappy. Her vision blurred with tears as she glanced down at Drew's screwed-up face. Maybe he was hungry.

Apparently, Hank had reached the same conclusion. Rifling through the diaper bag, he found a premixed bottle. He handed it to Mia, who silently offered the nipple to Drew. The baby stopped crying and grabbed on hungrily.

"T-thanks," she blubbered, frantically blinking back tears. While the baby drank, she moved uncertainly toward the door.

Hank caught her by the shoulders and turned her around, "Sit down," he ordered, setting her gently onto a chair.

She looked up at him. "B-but I want to go h-home. There are adoption files to read—"

"Not until the kid eats."

Too wretched and tired to argue she nodded. Hank sat beside her, his arm around her shoulders. Feeling foolish and vulnerable, she fed Drew in one arm and she leaned the other against Hank.

When the baby finished, Hank burped Drew. He spread his jacket on the floor and laid the boy on it. Then he returned to his chair.

"What are you doing? Drew finished his bottle." Mia pushed to her feet. "I'm ready to go home."

Gaping at her as if she'd lost her mind, Hank shook his head. "You're in no shape to go anyplace."

He was right. That started a fresh bout of tears. Sobbing like a fool but unable to stop, she sank back down. When he again settled his arm around her shoulders, she didn't protest.

HANK HAD SEEN Mia exhausted, worried and uncertain. But he'd never seen her like this, hunched into herself, arms hugging her middle, as bereft as if her heart had split in two. Watching her suffer hurt his chest.

Wishing he were anyplace but here, and at a loss for what to do, he shifted beside her. He couldn't turn his back on her now, when she needed comforting, needed a friend. He wasn't the best at either, but he'd try.

"Let it out, sweetheart," he soothed, pulling her closer to his side.

She was warm and pliant as she turned her face into his chest and did exactly that. In no time the front of his T-shirt was wet from her tears.

The rigid chairs didn't encourage sitting more than a few minutes. Hank's aching back and hip muscles begged him to stand and stretch. But helping Mia was more important than minor physical discomfort.

He rested his cheek on the top of her head. Her hair felt soft and smelled faintly of lemon. The fresh scent fit her.

"Tell me what's wrong," he urged, knowing he shouldn't ask. Best if he stayed out of it. Holding her was good enough.

She took in a shuddering breath, causing tiny flyaway tendrils to bounce like gentle caresses against his face.

"Not in front of Drew," she mumbled into his shirt.

He swore he could feel her lips against his heart. Sweet Lord. His body stirred to life.

"The kid's too little to understand," he managed to say.

He tightened his arm around her, gratified when she burrowed closer. Hardly aware of his actions, he closed his eyes and kissed the top of her head. If she turned her head a fraction and lifted her face, he could kiss her mouth.

He frowned. Mia was in pain and all he could think of was how her mouth would feel under his. What kind of one-track-mind jerk was he?

"You'll feel better if you share your troubles," he said.

He didn't really believe that, had never done it himself. But he figured it might work for Mia.

Raising her head, she looked up at him, her eyes very blue and very wet. "I wish I could, Hank, but I just c-can't."

With his thumb he wiped away the moisture clotting on her dark lashes. "Sure you can."

She pulled away. "You're such a good man. I don't know what I'd have done this morning without you." She sniffled. "And all I've done is yell at you. I'm s-so sorry."

He brushed the hair from her face the way his mother had when he was a kid. "No worries," he said. "You're upset about Drew." He offered what he hoped was an encouraging smile. "Anybody would be." Her gaze fastened onto his, and he knew she was listening. "The good news is, the little squirt is fine." He cupped her beautiful face in his hands and solemnly told her, "You'll be okay, too."

"Do you really believe that?"

"I sure do."

Her face was open, so full of pain and uncertainty and longing that he could no longer stop himself from doing what he'd fought against so many times.

He kissed her.

For a beat she hesitated and he thought he'd gone too far. Then she wrapped her arms around his waist and kissed him back. She tasted salty, like tears, and as warm and sweet as he remembered. Sweeter, because this time she was a participant.

Angling his head, he deepened the kiss, coaxing her lips apart. He tangled his tongue with hers. A low moan from deep in her throat vibrated through him, stirring the hunger that pulsed in his body.

He wanted her. Wanted to…

Drew let out a loud sound of complaint, interrupting the thought.

Breathing hard, Hank and Mia jerked apart. Her eyes had lost their haunted look. Instead, she stared dreamily at him, her cheeks flushed and her lips red, before she turned to Drew.

Hank stifled an oath. Kissing her had been a huge mistake. Because now, they both wanted more.

That wasn't going to happen. He wouldn't let it.

BY THE TIME Hank pulled Mia's tan station wagon into her driveway, half the morning was gone. Anxious to get to work and also to put some distance between him and Mia, he said his goodbyes as soon as he parked. The day was sunny and mild, and as he strode through the madronas to the site, bird sounds filled the air and squirrels chattered and scampered up and down trees.

He heard the voices of his six crew members before he saw them. The men were shirtless and hard at work on the upper story windows, a job that normally took half a day. But the design of this house called for more than the usual number of windows, with many of them huge and odd shaped. Handling and placing them properly was no easy task and would take days.

At first the men, intent on their jobs, didn't notice him. Nugget's joyous woof quickly alerted them, and they waved and called out.

Hank greeted Nugget, then climbed the ladder to the second floor, his hip protesting each step. The men had set and puttied seven windows. "You've made good progress this morning," he noted.

"That's 'cause we've been working like dogs," John Dixon said. At fifty-two, he was the oldest of the crew, and despite a sizable beer belly, the most skilled. "No offense, Nugget."

Bart Patterson, a strong and fit man in his early thirties—about Hank's age—turned to him. "These windows are a real pain. But they sure are pretty. This is the nicest house I ever worked on. You're sure to win that architecture prize."

Hank nodded and picked up a putty knife. "If that happens, it'll be thanks to all of you."

"That oughta put Forest Glen on the map," Pete Holmes said. Blond, buff, twenty-eight years old, he was the ladies' man of the group, always talking about his newest woman.

"Let's hope." Bart gave a thumbs-up. "Then we'll build more, each one just as pretty."

Hank shook his head. "My business is based in Seattle. I don't plan on staying here."

Del Farmer, a young, rangy man, exchanged a look with his equally young buddy, Tommy Smith. Both men glanced toward Mia's. "Maybe you'll change your mind," Del said.

Not wanting them to get the wrong idea about him and Mia, Hank quickly set them straight. "I'm her only neighbor. That's why I drove her and Drew to the hospital."

"How is the little guy?" Lester Leeds asked, grunting with the effort of positioning the pentagonal-shaped bathroom window. He and his wife had a toddler and a couple of grade-schoolers.

"Not a thing wrong with him," Hank replied.

Mia was a different story, though. Her heart seemed broken.

"Well, that's good," Bart said. "Sookie really was worried."

"New mom jitters. Told you." Del gave a sage

nod. "Kelly had 'em, too, after Abby was born." He helped Lester set the glass into its frame. "Every time our baby sneezed, Kelly was scared she had pneumonia. Course it wasn't nothin'." He grinned and shook his head. "Women."

As the men bantered about the fairer sex, Hank managed a comment now and then. But his mind was on other things.

Mia didn't want to be Drew's mother. She'd stated that several times over the past few days, including at the hospital this morning, and again, on the mostly silent drive home.

She was making a huge mistake, which she'd regret the rest of her life. But worried she'd start bawling again, Hank hadn't shared his opinion. Besides, what she did with her life wasn't his business.

Tell that to his heart.

"Mia's a good-lookin' woman," Pete commented.

Lester raised his bushy brows in Hank's direction. "You got a thing for her, Hank?"

Hank scowled. "Like I said, I'm her neighbor. Period."

Del and Tommy exchanged looks and Pete snickered.

Bart shrugged. "If you say so."

John wiped his sweaty brow with a meaty arm. "I'll tell you true. If I were younger, I'd go after her myself. Since Hank's not interested, maybe you should date her, Pete."

The other men grinned. Hank narrowed his eyes at Pete. If he or any of the men so much as looked at Mia…

"Chill, Hank." The blond man held up his hands, palms out. "She's not my type."

Hank nodded. He loosened his death grip on the putty knife. Dammit, he didn't want to care, couldn't afford the consequences. His body would repulse her, and he couldn't go through that again.

Then why in hell had he kissed her?

Because he'd lost his friggin' mind. At least now he was in control. He'd make sure he didn't see her or Drew anymore.

The men broke into raucous laughter. Hank didn't have a clue what the joke was, and with the heavy feeling in his chest he sure as hell didn't feel like laughing. Eager to prove to himself that he was in control, he pushed Mia and Drew from his thoughts and joined in anyway.

AS THE LAST patient, a border collie due for his annual shots, and his owner pulled out of Mia's driveway late Friday afternoon, she collapsed on the sofa.

Sookie let Ginger and Rags out of the kitchen where she'd enclosed them. Both animals bounded energetically toward Mia.

Leaning down, she rubbed Ginger's head and was rewarded with a lick on the chin. Rags jumped onto the cushion beside Mia, waiting until she leaned back. When she did, he settled on her lap, purring in contentment.

Stroking his back, she shook her head. "I thought today would never end."

"It was like a zoo, pun intended." Sookie sank onto the adjacent armchair. "I swear, over half the town has been here this week. And after today... All I can say is, I've never been so glad for a work week to end."

Somehow everyone knew that Drew would go to his new family on Monday. The very thought of his leaving gouged a hole in Mia's heart. People had also heard about this morning's trip to the emergency clinic.

She didn't want to think about *that*. Every time she did, she cringed. Crying out her heart to Hank was embarrassing enough. Then she'd made things worse by practically coercing him to kiss her. He'd done so out of pity. At least at first. She was certain the deep, attentive kisses that followed had been real.

The man sure could kiss. She released a dreamy sigh.

"Earth to Mia," Sookie said. "Where were you?"

Mia shook herself. "Somewhere in the ozone."

How she could fantasize about kissing Hank right

now was beyond her. She really didn't want to think at all, and she certainly didn't want to be alone.

She smiled at Sookie. "I know it's late, but do you have time for a glass of wine?"

Her friend shook her head. "Wish I could, but I'm not drinking." She winked. "Bart and I are trying to make a baby, remember?"

"Of course." Mia smiled wanly. "How could I forget? It's probably time to pick him up at Hank's, huh?"

Her emotions must have shown on her face. Sookie glanced at her watch, then shot her a concerned look. "He can wait a few minutes. You're having doubts, aren't you?"

No need to spell out the subject of those doubts. Drew was leaving. Oddly enough, he seemed to know. Since his visit to the hospital he'd been more demanding than ever, fussing nonstop and eating every two hours, until thirty minutes ago, thoroughly worn out, when at last he'd fallen asleep.

Despite taking care of him and seeing twenty patients, Mia had stuck to her decision to review the adoption files. During a brief lunch, leaving the baby with Sookie, she'd managed to read through the three files. She'd made her choice and had phoned the agency.

This was Drew's last weekend in Forest Glen.

Mia swallowed around the painful lump in her

throat. "I admit, the little guy has won my heart. But I want what's best for him. I picked out a good family." She didn't know their names yet, but they lived in Williamstown, Virginia. "They fly in Monday afternoon for the face-to-face interview. Then they'll take Drew."

And she'd never see him again, never cuddle or comfort him. It was the best choice for the baby, and she should have felt good about it. Instead her words hung in the air, leaving her cold, empty and feeling incredibly awful. She chafed her arms, but this kind of chill came from deep inside.

"Bart can catch a ride with Lester or Pete." Sookie patted Mia's knee. "I'll stay as long as you need me. Just let me phone him so he doesn't worry."

Much as Mia wanted her friend to stay, keeping her from her husband on a Friday night wasn't fair. Besides, her being here wouldn't change anything. She shook her head. "I'm ok—"

Suddenly the lights flickered. Then they went out. In the darkened room, she groaned. "Not again."

"First time this week," Sookie said.

"I swear, I'll upgrade the wiring in the next few weeks."

"Hey, don't worry. It's not quite dark yet, but it'll be easier with the flashlight." She got up to get it.

Mia shook her head. "This is a one-person job. You don't have to stay."

Once she reset the breakers, she'd watch television or pick up a good book. Anything to keep her mind off Monday.

"I want to. Once we fix the circuit breaker, I'll call Bart. He can walk over."

"Okay."

Mia and Sookie donned sweaters, and Mia slipped the baby monitor into her pocket. Drew wasn't likely to wake up for hours, but just in case…

Leaving the animals inside, they headed out. The air was cool and damp, but at least it wasn't raining.

Sookie aimed the bright halogen beam at the first breaker panel. Mia tripped every switch, but the cabin remained dark. Even though she knew the first panel was where the problem lay she repeated her actions with the second and third panel. In growing frustration, she tried the first again.

"It's no use," Sookie said. "We need help. I'll call Bart and ask him to bring Hank with him. Hank knows electrical stuff better."

After what had happened this morning? Embarrassed, Mia shook her head. "I can't ask Hank for help. I've bothered him way too much already. I—"

"It's no bother," Hank interrupted. Nugget stood at his side, tail wagging, and Bart was there, too. They'd come up so quietly the women hadn't noticed.

Mia's heart lifted and her cheeks warmed.

"Bart!" Sookie threw her arms around her husband. "Hello, honey."

Bart grinned, then kissed her. "You were late, so Hank and I decided to drop by."

Hank nodded at Mia, his eyes burning in the faint light. "What's the trouble?"

"You're just in time," Sookie said. "We blew a fuse and can't seem to fix it."

Hank slanted his head Mia's way again. "Weren't you going to update this mess?"

His gruff, scolding tone pricked. She bristled. "Yes, but lately I've had other things on my mind."

"I guess you have."

He glanced at her mouth and heat shot through her.

The two men conferred, then bent toward the breaker panels, Bart aiming the flashlight. Hank's broad shoulders strained his denim jacket. Under the jacket, Mia knew his body was hard and tapered slightly at the waist. She glanced at his rear end and long legs and pulled in a breath. His body was nicely proportioned. Okay, to die for.

Through the darkness, Sookie studied her with raised eyebrows. Mia shrugged. Her friend pulled the flashlight from Bart's hands and thrust it into hers.

"Time to go, hon. We'll leave Mia in Hank's capable hands."

Bart shot his wife a loving look. "Gotta do what the boss says, Hank. See you Monday."

"Good night, you two," Sookie said, grinning as she tugged her husband toward her car.

Chapter Nine

After fixing the blown breaker Hank shut the box and turned to Mia. Daylight had gone, but she was standing under the kitchen window, bathed in light from inside. Despite her drawn expression shapeless, bulky cardigan and loose slacks, she looked sexy and beautiful. And troubled.

He wasn't about to get further involved and he wasn't here to lust after her. He'd repeated a dozen times that he wasn't going to see her or Drew again, yet here he was, checking up on her and wanting her more than before. He was wading in dangerous waters.

"Your wires are in worse shape than I thought." He wiped his dirty hands on his Levi's. "I know somebody who can take care of this mess, a guy named Joe Sidell. He's the electrician I hired to do the wiring on my project."

"I know Joe." Mia fiddled with the flashlight,

flipping the switch on and off as if she were nervous. "His daughter owns a ferret I see now and then."

"I won't need him for another few weeks—and I happen to know he's hurting for work. Why don't I send him over on Monday?"

"That'd be great." She hugged the flashlight to her chest. "Only I won't be here Monday. That's when Drew and I go to the adoption agency in Bellingham to meet his new family."

Though her voice held steady, Hank heard the bleakness underneath.

"So you're really going to do it." His tone betrayed his opinion—that she was a damn fool.

Up came Mia's chin. "I told you that this morning."

"While you cried your heart out."

Giving up the baby she loved made no sense. She was hiding something that seemed to eat her up inside, but a gut instinct told Hank not to mention that. He wanted to know what it was, though. If he knew, maybe he could convince her to reconsider her decision.

No doubt about it, he wanted to help her. He shook his head at that, but he could no more stay out of her business and let her ruin her life than he could remove the scars from his body. Like it or not, he was involved.

"About that…" Pressing her fist to her mouth,

she glanced at the ground before aiming her gaze at him. "I'm a little embarrassed about breaking down in front of you."

"Hell, if you didn't, you'd have ice in your blood." He glanced at her mouth, the lips full and sweet. "There's nothing icy about you, Mia." He couldn't help asking, "What about those kisses? Did they embarrass you, too?"

Her gaze locked onto his. "No," she answered without hesitation. "Kissing you was exactly what I needed and what I wanted."

And exactly what Hank didn't want to hear. *Then why did you ask?* His mouth quirked. "Glad to be of help."

She returned a genuine smile that momentarily eclipsed her bleak expression and dazzled him.

Every nerve in his body tensed and strained toward her, urging him to pull her close and kiss her. He stifled a groan and shoved his hands, leash and all, into his hip pockets. She was killing him and she didn't even know it.

He needed to set her straight, let her know how things between them stood. Backing up a step, schooling his expression to neutral, he looked her straight in the eye. "I won't be doing that again. Kissing you."

She flushed. "I know you—"

His growling stomach cut off whatever she'd been

about to say. After an afternoon of hard, physical work, he was ravenous.

Mia shut her mouth and lowered her wide-eyed attention to his belly. "My goodness, that was as loud as a thunder clap."

She'd cracked a joke, breaking the tension. Relieved, Hank grinned and rubbed his empty gut. "Guess I'd better head home and feed it before it really gets out of hand."

"It won't be as good as last time," she said. "Just leftover meat loaf, succotash and a microwave potato. But there's plenty for both of us if you'd like to stay for dinner."

Tempting as the offer was, he hesitated. His feelings were a tangle of physical hunger and a need to help—a potentially dangerous combination.

If he were smart he'd head back to the safety of his trailer and push her from his thoughts. But the soft, pleading look on her face gripped him and wouldn't let go. This was her last weekend with Drew, a tough time to face alone. Who knew, maybe he'd coax her to open up and tell him the real reason she'd decided to give up the baby she loved. Then he could work on changing her mind.

He shrugged. "Why not?"

WHILE THE DOGS snored peacefully on the doggie bed and Rags curled up on living-room sofa—they knew Mia wouldn't feed them table scraps during dinner—she and Hank ate at the kitchen table. That is, Hank did. She wasn't hungry, and mostly pushed her food around the plate.

He scraped his plate clean for the second time, smacking his lips. "Another great dinner."

"I'm glad you liked it."

She could feel his curious gaze so she stabbed a forkful of baked potato and chewed it. Despite the sour cream and chives, it tasted like paste.

"Lost your appetite, huh?"

She swallowed. "Giving up Drew is hard."

"I can't even imagine." He shifted forward, his chair creaking. "Mia…"

By the way he said her name and the interested gleam in his slightly narrowed eyes, she knew a question would follow. Dreading it, she returned her attention to her plate. She'd wasted all that meat loaf. Gran was probably shaking her head from the grave.

"Look at me," Hank ordered in a soft but commanding tone she couldn't ignore.

Slowly she complied. His forearms rested on the table and his chin canted toward her.

"Do you want to finish my dinner?" she asked, knowing perfectly well this wasn't about food.

He wondered about her decision to give up Drew. She wasn't sure she could make sense of it without mentioning Gracie. But she'd never talked about what had happened, not after Gracie's death twenty-four years ago, and not in the years since then. First, because her family hadn't allowed it. Now, because the tragedy was behind her, left in the distant past where it belonged.

Hank shook his head. "I couldn't eat another bite, thanks."

She jumped up. "Well then, I'll just clear the table and put on the water for tea."

"Leave it." He clasped her wrist, stopping her. "Busywork won't fix your troubles, Mia. Talking them over with a friend might help."

His touch was firm and warm, yet gentle.

"Nobody can help," she said as she tried to pull free.

He wouldn't release her. Too tired and emotionally drained to fight, she sank back down.

His fingers slid to her hand and gave a reassuring squeeze. "Try me."

He cared about her, she realized. Otherwise he wouldn't offer to listen, wouldn't be here at all. She cared for him, too. The truth was, she was falling in love with him.

Love never lasted, so her feelings scared her. Telling him about the past frightened her more. What would he think of her then?

He was totally focused on her, his expression kind and encouraging. Maybe it was time to share the past, get it into the open. God knew, she'd locked it inside long enough. She pulled her hand from his and nodded.

"I, um…" Her throat felt as rusty as if she hadn't spoken for a month. She sipped her water, cleared her throat. "I've never talked about this before. This is difficult for me."

"I can deal with difficult."

Trust me. He didn't say it, but the sincerity and warmth in his eyes telegraphed the message as surely as if he'd spoken.

That was the push she needed. She blew out a heavy breath. "Once I had a baby sister. My parents and I waited a long time for her. She was born just after my fifth birthday. They named her Grace, because she arrived by the grace of God."

Hank's eyes widened slightly, but he didn't comment.

She went on. "In the mornings after my father left for work, it was my job to watch over Gracie while our mother showered. Gracie stayed in her crib and mostly slept, so I didn't do much. But I liked the responsibility. And though this may sound crazy, I think Gracie enjoyed it, too." She paused, smiling at the faint memory of the baby's guileless eyes and toothless grin. "One morning, when she was barely three months old, I was watching over her the same as always. Only this time something went wrong."

Pain washed over Mia like a slow-moving wave. For some reason, she couldn't look directly at Hank. She scratched at a dried milk stain on the sleeve of her blouse. "My little sister died of SIDS—sudden infant death syndrome."

Through her lowered lashes, she saw him flinch and knew he felt her misery.

"I'm sorry," he said in a voice laced with sympathy.

Mia swallowed. "It was terrible."

"Listen, if this is too much to talk about…"

Now that she'd started, she couldn't stop. She stared straight into his unwavering gaze. "I need to tell you."

He nodded, and she continued. "Gracie's death tore my family apart. My father couldn't get past it. He left us six months later and headed up to the Alaskan wilderness. My mother could barely function, and soon after he left, she couldn't handle taking care of me. She dropped me off here with my gran. Neither of them ever came back."

Hank looked incredulous. "But you were their only other child. Why would they abandon you?"

"Don't you see?" The answer was so clear that Mia scoffed. "Gracie's death was my fault."

There. The secret was out.

Bracing for Hank's condemnation, she straightened her spine. The outrage she saw surprised her.

"They blamed you?" Eyes blazing, hands balled into fists, he swore.

His anger on her behalf was misplaced, but somehow made her feel better. "Nobody actually said it was my fault. In fact we never discussed what had happened and never again said Gracie's name out loud. My parents wouldn't allow it. Neither would Gran. She said to put the past behind me, and I did."

"Since it's been eating away at you all these years, apparently you didn't."

Mia hadn't realized that until now. The insight astonished her. "Anyway, now you know why I have to give up Drew. Babies aren't safe in my care."

"You don't honestly believe that."

When she shrugged, Hank gaped at her as if she had two heads. "You're a vet, Mia. You know that now and then animals die before their time. It happens."

She nodded. "But—"

"But nothing," he interrupted. "Gracie's death was heartbreaking, but nobody's fault. Certainly not yours. Sudden infant death syndrome can happen in any family."

Of course, he was right. "I realize that," she said. *But that applies to* other *people.*

"Then you also know her death had nothing to do with you. It wasn't your fault," he repeated, with such feeling that she truly heard.

The absolute certainty shining from his eyes added to the meaning of his words. She stared wide-eyed at him. He was right.

Gracie's death, tragic as it was, was *not her fault*.

The heavy darkness deep inside her opened and shifted, and suddenly she felt lighter than air. "Oh, Hank." She laughed and cried at the same time. "I think…I think maybe you're right."

"Damn straight, I am." His mouth quirked as he offered a gratified nod. "And I'm glad you know it." A full grin bloomed across his face, making him look breathtakingly handsome.

Hope stirred in her. Hugging her waist, she voiced her biggest fear. "You really believe I could raise Drew without hurting him?"

He chuckled softly, the sound as warm and bright as the afternoon sun. "Sweetheart, I'd stake my own life on it. Why don't you call that adoption agency and tell them you've changed your mind?"

Mia wanted to, more than anything. But she'd carried the blame for Gracie's death for so long. Even though she could see that she wasn't responsible, even though Hank believed in her, the old doubts were difficult to shake.

"I want to think about it awhile longer."

"Do you think it's fair for the adoptive family to come all this way, expecting to take home a baby, when you might change your mind?"

"No," she said.

He nodded. "You'd best decide damn soon."

HANK WAS AWED that Mia had shared her past with him. He also was furious with her family. Piling heavy guilt on a five-year-old kid when it wasn't her fault and then abandoning her—that turned his stomach. He wished her parents and grandma were alive so he could shake all three of them.

Small wonder Mia was plagued with self-doubt. He wanted to crush her guilt so she'd stop chewing on her bottom lip and fidgeting with her napkin, so she'd pick up the phone and call the adoption agency right now.

He didn't know how to erase the shadows, but he was damned if he'd leave here tonight without one more attempt at it.

"You'll make a great mom," he said. "No, you already *are* a great mom."

"Thanks, Hank. I just hope you're right." She offered a fleeting smile, but her eyes were uncertain. "That is, if I decide to adopt Drew."

This time when she rose to stack the plates, he didn't stop her. Instead he joined her, piling the vegetable bowl on top of the empty meat loaf platter.

"I don't say something unless I mean it. I've watched you handle Drew. Nobody could be more loving or nurturing."

"That means a lot." She set the plates on the counter next to the sink and turned to him, her face bright with hope. "These past few weeks you've been so wonderful to me. I'm glad you came into my life."

He set the serving dishes next to the plates, then shuffled his feet in discomfort. "Uh, thank you."

"No, thank you!" She threw her arms around him, nearly knocking him over.

Caught off guard, he laughed and staggered backward with her, widening his stance to keep from falling over. His arms circled her waist and her familiar lemon scent tickled his senses. She only came up to his chin, so he spoke to the crown of her head. "You're very welcome."

"Mmm, you feel good." She snuggled closer.

He tightened his grasp. "So do you."

Holding her was tempting fate, but he couldn't let her go just yet. He closed his eyes and for one long moment savored the feel of her round breasts against his chest and her lower body tantalizing his groin. Surely she felt his arousal.

Let her go! his mind warned. And still he held her.

She cupped his shoulders and slanted her head back to look at him. There was no mistaking the desire on her face as she searched his eyes.

"What you said earlier about not kissing me again—you didn't mean it, did you?"

"I thought I did," he murmured. "But right now, holding you, all I want is to taste you again."

Her eyelids dropped to half-mast. "What are you waiting for?" Rising on her toes, she offered her mouth.

Her lashes were sooty against her pale cheeks. Her lips were pink and plump and waiting. *His.*

He claimed them.

Her mouth opened to accept his tongue. As he deepened the kiss, she moaned, as eager and hungry as she'd been this morning.

Hank wanted her more than he'd ever wanted a woman. He was at full attention now, hard and pulsing and hot. He cupped her hips and brought her tightly against his erection. She squirmed against the sensitive length, making him drunk with pleasure.

He was about to lose his mind. He slid his hands up her sides to her breasts, pleased when she angled back a fraction to give him the access he sought.

Groaning, he cupped both full breasts, flexing his hands around their soft heaviness. Despite the barriers of her bra and blouse, he felt her nipples tighten.

Mia broke the kiss. Eyes locked on his, breathing shallow and rapid, she unbuttoned her shirt and slipped out of it. Her plain, white bra was a stark contrast against the flush on her neck and chest. It wasn't see-through, low-cut or sexy, and yet the points of her nipples poking the cotton was incredibly erotic. Hank wanted to see her breasts. He reached for the front clasp, then stopped with a questioning look.

"Yes," she said.

He nodded and unhooked it, tossing it aside.

Her breasts were large and full, her nipples rosy. "Lovely," he murmured.

He lifted her onto the counter, not far from the dishes. Standing between her thighs, he reverently took one tip into his mouth and ran his tongue over the stiff peak. Soft moans broke from her throat. Sweet Christmas. She tasted better than in his wildest fantasies. While he nipped and licked and laved her breasts, her thighs gripped his hips.

Suddenly she pushed his head away. "My turn."

Breathing hard, she reached for the hem of his shirt. And common sense took over. Once she saw the scars....

He circled her wrists and stopped her. "Don't." Realizing he sounded gruff, he softened his tone. "Let me pleasure you tonight. Only you."

"But that's not fair." She smiled with lips red and slightly swollen from his kisses, her eyes dark with desire. "Let's pleasure each other."

While his body screamed for exactly that, he shook his head. "No."

He removed her legs from his hips and backed away, silently mourning the loss of contact and warmth.

Mia's forehead wrinkled and her eyes clouded. "What's wrong?"

Her shirt lay in a heap on the floor. Her bra hung

haphazardly over the back of a kitchen chair. He retrieved both and handed them to her. "This was a bad idea."

"You didn't think so a minute ago." Ignoring the bra, she slipped into the blouse and buttoned it. "I thought you wanted this."

He glanced at her perky nipples, clearly visible under the blouse, and swallowed. "I do." Way too much.

"Then why did we stop?"

Unwilling to explain, he plowed a hand through his hair. "It's complicated."

"No, it isn't." She slid off the counter and tugged the blouse over her hips. "Either you want me or you don't." Arms crossed over her chest, she regarded him with an expectant look.

She wanted a reason. Hank swore, shifted uncomfortably and rubbed the back of his neck. He didn't explain. Couldn't.

Mia gave a terse nod. The hurt on her face made his own chest ache.

"I understand now," she said. "You feel sorry for me because of what I told you. That's the only reason you kissed me and touched me."

She had it all wrong. "Look, Mia—"

"Don't make things worse by lying to me, Hank." She was angry now, eyes flashing and chin high. Turning her now stiff back on him, she strode to the hooks beside the back door, where Nugget's and Ginger's leashes hung side-by-side. "I think you'd better leave." She handed him Nugget's leash, then, tight-lipped, opened the door.

He snapped the leash onto his dog's collar and followed the animal out. "Good night."

The door slammed behind him.

Chapter Ten

Hard physical labor always cleared Hank's mind, and after what had just happened, he needed to shut off his thoughts. But it was too dark to work on the house. So he paced the small trailer and damned himself for ignoring reason and kissing Mia. Again.

His last look at her, her eyes hot with anger and distress, haunted him. He'd set out to help her. Instead he'd hurt her.

"You really screwed things up this time," he muttered.

At his heels, Nugget whined softly.

In no mood for the dog's sympathy, he scowled. "Go away, mutt."

The animal tucked his tail between his legs and slunk out of the room. Dammit, this wasn't the dog's fault. Hank felt worse than ever. "I'm sorry," he called.

He was halfway to the hall where Nugget had gone when the phone rang, shrill in the silence.

Hoping it was Mia, he sprinted into the kitchen and picked up before the second ring.

"Wow, that was fast. Expecting somebody special?"

It was his brother, Jake. They hadn't spoken since Christmas, and then only about surface things—the food, the weather, football. Hank had kept it that way. He knew that otherwise the conversation would turn to Gil's death or Hank's lack of female company, which was nobody's business. Even with impersonal conversation, the family tended to smother him in pity, so he mostly steered clear of them. But a few nights ago, after talking to his parents, he'd left a message on Jake's machine.

"Hey, Jake."

"Got your voice mail. What's up?"

Hearing his brother's voice brightened Hank's spirits, but he wasn't a man to share his feelings. "Not much." He carried the portable to the sofa and sank onto it. "How're you?"

"Good. Still running the computer store. You?"

"Doing fine." As long as he didn't think about Mia and their fight tonight. He pushed the thought from his mind.

Nugget strolled in and nosed his thigh. The dog had forgiven the outburst. Hank scratched the hard-to-reach place behind his head. "You should see this house I'm building, bro."

"Mom and Dad say you're hoping to win the Architectural Award of the West. Gil was one hell of a talented man."

"He sure was. That's why I'm bustin' my hump here in Podunk, U.S.A. He knew what he was doing when he chose this location. The setting is perfect for the house. We're sure to win."

"Good to hear you thinking like that. You weren't so positive last time we talked."

Wary of the statement, Hank frowned into the phone. He let go of Nugget. The dog lay at his feet, head propped on Hank's boot. "Watch it, Jake. I don't need a pep talk and I don't want you feeling sorry for me."

His brother blew out a loud breath, then swore, and Hank pictured him, jaw clamped as he shot a frustrated glance at the ceiling. "All I want is to be there for you, like you were for me during the divorce."

Hank had practically lived with his brother during his nasty divorce. They always had been close—until the accident. After that he'd shut out Jake, refusing to let his brother or anyone else into his private hell. Now he saw that his withdrawal had hurt his brother. He was sorry, but didn't know how to apologize.

"I know, bro. I appreciate that, and I'm glad you're there." Feeling awkward over the admission, he changed the subject. "How's everybody else?"

Jake filled him in on Lisa, Ryan and their kids. "We'd all like to see you," he finished.

"Yeah? I'd like to see you guys, too, but I can't stand that nobody can relax around me. You all act like you're afraid I'll break down, or worse." He sensed tension and leaned forward, frowning. "It's true, and you know it."

"Ever stop to figure out the real reason everyone's tense when you're here?"

Hank narrowed his eyes. "What in hell are you trying to say?"

"You asked, so here it is. I don't pity you, Hank. Nobody in this family does. We don't hold you responsible for the accident, either. Even Gil's family knows it wasn't your fault. If you'd just accept it and move on, we wouldn't all feel like we're walking on eggshells when you're around."

Wasn't your fault. Not your fault. Hank had heard it before and had always rejected the statement as a feeble platitude. Now it reverberated in his head, mainly because he'd said those very words to Mia earlier tonight—after she'd told him about Gracie's death. He didn't figure they applied to him. Now he considered the possibility.

The truck driver who'd plowed into the car had fallen asleep at the wheel. True, if Hank had been sober and driving, he'd have taken a different route. True, he was more than sorry about what happened, and he missed Gil something awful.

But his death wasn't Hank's fault.

Beginning to accept the truth of it, he shook his head.

"Hank?" Jake prodded. "You're awfully quiet. Did you hang up on me?"

"Nope." Feeling as if he'd dropped a one-ton load from his shoulders, he quietly added, "Thank you."

"What'd I do?" His brother sounded surprised.

"Oh, nothing much. Just kicked my sorry ass when I needed it."

"Huh?"

Hank could imagine his brother's confusion. His mouth quirked. "I'll explain some other time. Why don't you and the rest of the family come for a visit? It's a two-hour drive from Seattle, but the scenery is great. Tomorrow or Sunday works for me."

"Tomorrow, then. I'll bring my honey."

"Whoa." It was Hank's turn to be surprised. "Last time we talked you'd barely started dating again. Who is she?"

"Her name's Jeannie Cochran and she teaches first grade. We met at a Laundromat, of all places, back in October. I just didn't tell the family for a while. Didn't want that pressure. You know what I mean."

Though Jake couldn't see him, Hank nodded. "I sure do."

"She's something special."

He grinned into the phone. "Sounds serious."

"You got that right. I'm thinking about shocking Mom, Dad and myself, and asking her to marry me. But I'm not telling anyone but you, so keep it quiet."

"Scout's honor." Hank was happy for his brother, yet also envious. "Congratulations."

His thoughts drifted to Mia. She was special, too. He easily could fall for her. But he wasn't cut out for love, especially with his sorry mess of a body.

"Can't wait for you to meet her," Jake said. "I'll check with the parents and everybody else about tomorrow."

Hank liked that idea. He gave his brother directions, then asked, "You coming for lunch?"

Suddenly, Nugget's head jerked up. He scrambled to his feet and trotted to the door, whining.

"Hang on, Jake."

Hank heard the shrieks of some kind of alarm. Mia was his only neighbor. Carrying the phone, he moved quickly to the door. As soon as he opened it, he smelled smoke. His heart jumped into his throat.

"What's that noise?" Jake asked.

"No time to explain," Hank replied. "Catch you later."

"Now that you've burped, let's change your diaper," Mia told Drew as she carried him from the kitchen to his room.

She laid him on the changing table and unsnapped

his sleeper. His big, round eyes followed her, and she swore he looked pleased. Her heart expanded with love. She kissed his round little tummy. "You are so cute," she cooed as she removed his soiled diaper.

He blew bubbles at her and kicked his plump legs. Oh, how she loved him. Her very soul yearned to nurture and raise him as her own. *If* she could keep him safe. She still wasn't convinced.

But she *was* leaning that way. She cleaned and dried his dimpled little bottom, knowing she wouldn't have even dared to hope if not for Hank. She hadn't realized how badly she'd needed to talk about Gracie. Hank had encouraged her to open up, and had listened without judgment. More important, he'd helped her understand a truth she should have figured out long ago but hadn't been able to grasp: that she was not responsible for Gracie's death or for the disintegration of her family. Mia was beyond grateful to him.

She was also in love with him. Which was a huge and sad joke.

Lifting Drew's legs, she slid a clean diaper under him, then fastened it. Of course Hank liked her. That was obvious. But he wasn't attracted to her. She'd thought maybe he was but she'd been wrong. Yes, he'd kissed her and touched her and showed her a glimpse of heaven. But he did those things because he knew she wanted him and he felt sorry for her.

Not because he desired her. The rejection stung. Remembering, she felt her cheeks warm. How embarrassing.

No, she wasn't going to waste one more moment thinking about Hank.

She snapped Drew into a clean sleeper. "What do you think, sweetie? Would I make a good mommy for you?"

The baby gurgled happily.

Mia's heart melted, and she grinned like an idiot. "I take that as a yes." Her smile faded and she bit her lip. "But I want what's best for you. I need to sleep on this, okay?" Though with the weighty decision on her mind, sleep was doubtful.

As she picked him up and propped him on her shoulder, she smelled smoke. She wrinkled her nose. *Odd.* "Maybe I left a burner on or—"

Ginger's frantic barks interrupted her. The dog met her in the hallway, bounding forward in her awkward three-legged trot. She nosed Mia's thigh, then limp-raced to the kitchen, where Rags pawed the door like a dog begging to get out.

All stove burners were off. Worry prickled the back of Mia's neck. She frowned. "Is Hank burning something tonight?"

He'd never done that before. She opened the door and sniffed. "I don't smell it out here."

Rags shot outside. Ginger glanced from the

darkness beyond to Mia, clearly wanting to leave but torn between deserting her and racing into the night.

The second Mia closed the door, the smoke alarm started to shriek. She jumped, startling Drew. His face puckered and he let out a wail.

"It's okay," she soothed over the annoying clangs as she hurried through the house, seeking out the source of the smoke.

Not the living room, not the bathroom, not Drew's room. Her bedroom at the end of the hall was the last room she checked. The air was hazy. Thin wisps of smoke oozed from the crack between the floor molding and the wall. Had to be the wiring.

Oh, why hadn't she updated it?

Squalling baby in her arms, she slammed the bedroom door and raced toward the kitchen. Once there, she called 9-1-1, shouting over the alarm, Drew's cries and Ginger's frantic barking.

The fire department, made up of volunteers, would take a good thirty minutes to arrive. By then…

Over the noise she heard a loud *pop!* just as the lights in the back of the house shut off.

Hank, she thought, *I need you.* But their earlier fight still smarted, and her pride wouldn't let her call him. She grabbed the diaper bag, which because she'd been too busy to empty it, still contained everything she needed to take with her for now. She snatched an old sweater from the rack by the door.

Ginger at her heels and Drew in her arms, she ran outside.

"Come, Ginger," she commanded as she hurried to her car.

She strapped Drew into his car seat, the only safe place she could think of. Mindful of the chill night air and the doctor's advice about keeping him warm, she tucked the sweater around the boy. It was way too big, too bulky, but there was no time to find a baby blanket. He was still crying, but she couldn't worry about that now.

"Stay with Drew," she ordered Ginger. She shut them both in the car.

Smoke billowed from the back of the house but there were no flames. The fire hadn't burst through the walls yet.

The clinic. It was on the opposite side of the cabin with separate wiring, but that was no guarantee it was safe. Two animals were in there, the hawk and a Siamese cat with a nasty respiratory infection. She had to get them out. The quickest route was through the living room.

Heart pounding, nerves on edge, she raced toward the front door. Abruptly all the lights at that end of the cabin went out and the alarm fell silent. Mia stumbled in the sudden darkness and pitched forward. Hands cupped her arms firmly from behind, saving her from a fall.

She knew that touch. She spun around, and there Hank stood, as if her earlier thoughts had summoned him. She was more than relieved to see him, and his name sang from her lips like the answer to a prayer. "Hank." Smoke tickled her throat and she coughed. Eyes smarting, pride and hurt forgotten, she grasped the sleeves of his denim jacket. "You're here."

A loud breath shot from his throat. "Thank God you're all right." He pulled her into a quick hug, then pushed back. "Where's Drew?"

"In the car, strapped into his car seat. Ginger's with him."

"Smart thinking. I shut off the power."

That explained the darkness. She couldn't see, but that wasn't about to stop her. She had to rescue the animals. "Give me your flashlight." Snatching it from Hank, she rushed up the front step.

"Wait a minute." He snagged her wrist, stopping her. "You shouldn't go back in there. It's not safe."

Smoke billowed from the back of the house as if to underlie the statement.

"I don't have a choi—"

A paroxysm of coughs cut off her words. Swearing, Hank tugged her away from the smoke. She twisted and tried to get free, but he held fast.

"The animals," she choked.

"How many and where are they?"

"Clinic. The hawk in the recovery room and a cat

in the sick room. There's a fire extinguisher in the utility room."

"Can you hold your breath long enough to run in, grab it and run out?"

She nodded. "I'll go through the kitchen."

"Do it, and I'll take care of the animals."

"You'll need this." She thrust the flashlight at him.

He shoved it into his rear pocket, then shrugged out of his jacket and tossed it aside. Moving quickly, he pulled off his T-shirt on the way inside and held it over his nose and mouth. He disappeared in the smoke.

Mia hurried to the back of the house in time to see the first tendrils of red-orange flame lick the outside wall between her room and Drew's.

Dear God. Sucking in a huge breath, she darted inside. The kitchen was smoky but not on fire. At least, she didn't believe so. The room was pitch-black, but having lived here most of her life, she moved with ease through it to the utility room. She grabbed the fire extinguisher and her own flashlight and hurried out.

Once outside she gulped in air, choking and sputtering from the smoke. Flashlight in her mouth, she worked the pin on the fire extinguisher. Hank's flashlight beam caught her attention. Shining the light in front of him, keeping to the dark, he set a cage on the ground—away from the smoke and near the car.

"Thanks," she called.

Coughing and holding the shirt to his chest as if he were too shy to show his bare torso, he threw her a thumbs-up. Then he disappeared around the front of the house.

Mia aimed the sprayer. Foam shot out, hissing as it spit at the flames. While she tried to dampen the fire, Hank emerged with the cat cage. He set it on the other side of the car, well out of the way of the hawk and the smoke. He peered briefly at Drew, then slipped his T-shirt over his head, tugging it down as he came toward her.

"Drew's asleep. I think the animals are okay. The clinic isn't smoky, and I saw no signs of fire."

"That's something to be grateful for," Mia said.

Hank took the extinguisher from her and nudged her aside. "The lights in the clinic were still on." He sprayed a vicious flame, beating it back. "I shut off the power and closed the door. Hopefully that'll cut down on the smoke damage. That's *if* the fire doesn't destroy everything." He emptied what was left at the flames. "Any refills for this thing?"

She shook her head.

His nod was brief. "Nothing to do now but wait for the fire department, and pray they get here in time."

SOMETIME around eleven, the fire department at last killed the fire. Hank was as grimy and sweaty as the eight firefighters who, out of concern for his safety, hadn't let him near the cabin. Wishing he could do more but feeling powerless, he'd stuck close to Mia in case she needed him. God knew, he needed to be near her.

She could have died in that fire, along with Drew. He'd almost lost them. The thought nearly brought him to his knees. Profoundly grateful for her escape but unable to express his feelings, he stood beside her, silently offering comfort as they took in the damage—along with Sookie, Bart and a half-dozen people who had materialized as the night wore on. One way or another each had supported Mia. Feeding, diapering and entertaining Drew. Keeping Ginger safe and out of the way. Comforting Rags. Providing coffee and sandwiches.

The headlights from two fire trucks illuminated the mess of charred wood and chemical foam in the gaping holes that had been the bedrooms and bathroom. In eerie contrast, the toilet, bathroom sink and bathtub gleamed stark white.

By some miracle, the fire had ignored the rest of the cabin and the clinic. Several firefighters had walked through both sections, making a thorough check of every room. Though they found smoke damage, together with a middle-aged woman named Martha Hicks, Mia's insurance agent, they estimated she could reopen the clinic in approximately one week. Rebuilding and cleaning the cabin, though, would take longer.

She'd been through so much with Drew, and now this. Yet she stood undefeated and undaunted, head up and baby secure in her arms. Hank both marveled at and admired her strength. She was a heck of a lot stronger than he'd ever be.

As Mia set up a meeting for the following day with her insurance agent, then thanked the other townspeople and the exhausted men, Sookie squeezed her arm. She shot a curious look at Drew, and Hank figured she was about to ask whether Mia had changed her mind and decided to keep him. He wanted to know, too. Judging by the other interested glances, so did everybody else.

However Mia's friend didn't ask. The others had the good grace to keep quiet, too. This probably wasn't the best time to bring up the pending adoption, and anyway they'd all know soon enough.

"Bart and I don't have much room, but you and Drew are welcome to stay with us," Sookie offered.

Mia opened her mouth, but Hank beat her to it. "Thanks, but they're staying with me."

Everybody nodded and smiled, especially Sookie and Bart. Sookie shrugged. "That's settled, then."

Mia shot Hank a look he couldn't interpret. "Are you sure? Your place is smaller than theirs. I don't want to put you out."

"I have room," he said. To put a stop to the knowing, male smirks he added, "The sofa folds out into a Hide-A-Bed." He'd take that and give Mia and Drew his more comfortable bed.

Looking undecided, she glanced at the caged animals nearby. "I'll put the hawk in the flight cage out back, but what about the cat? I can't just leave him outside."

"I'll take him home," Sookie volunteered. "First thing tomorrow I'll call Mrs. Dowell and ask her to pick him up here. I'll bring him back when I come in the morning."

"But tomorrow's Saturday," Mia said. "You heard what these guys said." She gestured at the firefighters. "There's smoke damage. I won't be able to see patients for at least a week."

"I don't care what day of the week it is or when you reopen for business," Sookie replied. "You need help putting things in order, and I intend to be there with my sleeves rolled up and a load of cleaning supplies. I'm happy to help with Drew, too."

Mia offered a grateful smile, then, mindful of the baby, pulled her assistant into a one-armed hug. "Thanks, Sookie. You're a true friend. But we can't do a thing until Martha assesses the damage in daylight."

"That'll be at ten o'clock tomorrow," the insurance agent said. "Don't plan on starting repairs until next week."

Mia nodded. "See?" she told Sookie. "It's fine to take the weekend off."

Several people spoke at once. "I'll stop by Monday morning."..."Count me in."..."I know you'd do the same for me."

Visibly overcome by their offers to help, Mia swallowed. "Thank you all, so much."

The generosity and love these people had for her amazed Hank. She had yet to agree to spend the night in his trailer, and since he didn't want anybody else offering her a place to sleep, he pushed. "I'm your closest neighbor in ten miles. It makes good sense to stay with me, so you're close to the clinic."

"All right, but just for tonight. Tomorrow I'll find a place to rent until I can rebuild the cabin."

He was simultaneously pleased and ticked at himself. He wanted Mia. Having her in the trailer was dangerous. But at least he'd know she and Drew were safe.

"Call me tomorrow, when you get the chance," Sookie said. She and Bart retrieved the caged cat. Mia's friends said their goodbyes and left.

The volunteer firefighters, tired but keyed up from the adrenaline rush of battling the fire, stuck around. They chatted with Mia about how to handle the smoke damage, and filled out papers she'd need for her insurance company. During the conversation Mia cuddled Drew, who was tired and cranky. Eventually the firefighters drifted back to their vehicles and drove off.

Leaving Hank alone with her in the chilly night.

"You sure have a lot of friends," he said.

"More than I ever realized," she replied with astonishment. "People around here are gossipy and nosy, but in a time of need, they're the best."

Hank had loaned her his jacket hours ago, yet she shivered. She tucked the bulky sweater around the baby. In the sudden silence between them, he dug the toe of his boot into the dirt. He wanted to ask about Drew, to tell her how much he admired her strength, to pull her close and show her how relieved he was that she was all right.

Instead he jerked his flashlight toward the madronas. "Ready to go?"

"I will be, once I take care of the hawk." She trained her flashlight near the bird. "Will you take him to the flight cage?"

Grunting, he hefted the cage. The thing weighed a ton. Earlier, adrenaline pumping, he hadn't noticed.

Mia had planned to carry it out of the clinic, through the smoky house. She'd never have made it. Sickened by the thought, he shuddered. "How did you think you could possibly carry this thing out of the clinic?" he asked in a tone brusque with fear.

The hawk shrieked, and Drew let out a distressed

wail. Mia shot Hank an irritated frown. "Keep your voice down," she warned softly. "You're scaring the bird and upsetting the baby."

Hank cleared his throat. "You could have died," he accused in a loud whisper.

Her back straightened. "I'm not helpless, Hank. I would have managed."

Tight-lipped, his back and hip protesting the awkward weight of the cage, he followed Mia's beam of light to the large flight cage behind the clinic.

Juggling Drew, she unlatched the wire gate. "Put the whole cage inside."

That didn't make sense. He frowned. "You're not going to let him out?"

His sharp tone earned him a look of exasperation. "What is your problem?"

I almost lost you tonight and I can't handle that. "It just seems cruel."

"Well, it's not. His damaged wing isn't ready. In this bigger space he'll want to fly. That could cause permanent damage."

"Why put him in here at all?" Hank asked as he grudgingly set the heavy cage inside.

"Because we can't leave him in the clinic. At least locked in here he'll be safe from predators." She shut and latched the door.

Hank wiped his hands on his jeans and turned to

go. Mia stayed put, absently cuddling Drew while she stared into space. What was she seeing and thinking?

She'd had one hell of a day. She must be wiped out, both emotionally and physically. And here he was, snapping at her every chance he got, when what he really wanted was to pull her close and never let her go.

Feeling like an insensitive jerk, he touched her shoulder. "It's time to head for the trailer."

"I know." Pivoting, she took a last, wistful look at the charred back of the cabin. She blew out a sigh and glanced at Hank. "I'm ready now."

Chapter Eleven

Aiming the flashlight beam on the ground, diaper bag slung on his shoulder, Hank headed for the trees accompanied by Mia, Drew and her pets.

Mia kept pace beside him, solemn and silent, holding the baby against her chest.

Hank glanced at her. "From beginning to end, it's been a rough day. How're you holding up?"

"You mean, considering I just lost part of my home?" She shook her head. "I don't think I've quite digested that yet."

Having been through a few emotional traumas of his own, Hank understood. If she felt bitter and angry, he wouldn't blame her. He nodded but said nothing. Neither did she, and for a long moment the only sounds were the creek babbling in the distance and the rustle of their shoes against the damp grass.

Finally she let out a soft sigh. "At least Drew and

the animals are alive and unhurt." Her hand smoothed over the infant's little back. "And fire didn't touch the clinic or the kitchen, utility or living rooms. I still have my gran's recipe box and the old andirons her grandfather forged for her when she built the cabin. I'd have to say, I'm more thankful than anything else."

Her ability to place the good in her life over the bad awed him. "I admire your positive attitude," he said. "The most positive thing of all is that tonight you more than proved you can keep Drew safe."

His words lightened her expression. "I did, didn't I?"

He shot her a sideways look. "Now that you know he's safe with you, are you going to raise him?"

"Yes." She nodded without hesitation.

"That's great." He shot her a triumphant grin.

She returned the grin. "I have the home number for Mrs. Pearson the agency. I'll call her first thing in the morning."

"Call tonight."

"But it's too late. I'll wake her up."

"Your decision is worth a wake-up call."

She nodded. "You're right."

"That's my girl." He slipped his arm around her shoulders and tugged her close.

"Don't, Hank."

Posture rigid, she pulled away as if she couldn't

stand to touch him. That hurt like a son of a bitch, but he'd been through it before with Kristin.

Only, Mia's reaction stemmed from anger and hurt over what had happened after those kisses earlier tonight. She thought he didn't want her. If she only knew…

He swallowed, wondering how to make up with her without revealing his reasons for pulling back physically. Call him a coward, but he wasn't going there.

How to explain? Unfortunately his mind came up blank, and they walked the rest of the way in stony silence.

Once they reached his property he shut Ginger inside the dog run, where Nugget waited, wagging his tail. The animals retreated into the doghouse.

In the trailer Hank loaned Mia a sweatshirt and sweatpants to sleep in. While she showered and Drew lay sleepy but awake atop the sweater she'd spread on the floor, Hank made up the Hide-A-Bed and changed the sheets on his bed.

When he returned to the living room Drew was antsy and fussy. Hank picked him up. Recalling what had soothed his niece and nephew at the same age, he smoothed his hand over the baby's round little head and made low noises. Drew cocked his head toward Hank's voice, but refused to be comforted. Even with his face scrunched, ready to cry, he was cute. Hank jiggled him gently against his chest. The boy turned toward his heart, his mouth open and searching.

"I guess you're hungry, huh?"

The kid was full-out bawling now.

"Hang on, squirt."

Hank laid him back on the sweater. Quickly he retrieved the diaper bag he'd set on the coffee table. The can of powdered formula and a clean bottle were on top. He made up the bottle as fast as he could, then picked up Drew and carried him to the lone armchair. He settled into it, his knees hitting the mattress of the made-up Hide-A-Bed. The baby latched onto the nipple. His eyes fixed on Hank's face and his tiny hand touched Hank's cheek.

Emotion swelled in his chest. So much had happened in Drew's short life, yet the kid just hung in there and demanded what he needed. Hank really liked the little guy, who was as tenacious and tough as his mother.

"Tonight you're one very lucky kid," he said in a gruff voice.

While Drew sucked down his meal, Mia emerged, looking clean and fresh. Her hair was wet and the socks he'd loaned her flopped loosely. His sweats were equally huge on her. Yet though he couldn't see a single curve, he thought she looked sexy as hell in his clothes.

"Thanks for feeding Drew." She deposited her sooty clothes in the corner. "I'll take over."

As she reached for the baby, her pants slid down. With the sweatshirt hanging halfway to her thighs, Hank couldn't see so much as a glimpse of leg. He wished he'd given her a shorter shirt.

Red-faced, Mia grabbed the waistband and hauled the pants up. "I'd better sit down first."

She sat on the bed and leaned against the back cushions.

Hank handed her the baby. "Sorry I don't have smaller clothes."

"Hey, these are better than nothing."

He pictured her naked and his gaze combed hungrily over her body. "I don't know about that."

The eyes that jerked to his flashed surprise, then anger. "We both know you're not interested, so don't pretend otherwise."

"It was only a joke," he said.

"Well, it wasn't funny." Her mouth firmed into a thin line.

The very air felt tense and almost as thick as the smoke during the fire. Hank rocked back on his heels. He thought about telling her the truth—that he wanted her, but he was afraid of her rejection.

"No more jokes," he said, and she gave a terse nod. "I changed the sheets on my bed for you and Drew. I'll sleep out here."

A sigh issued from her lips and her anger seemed to dissolve in weary resignation. Without meeting his eye, she shook her head. "You've done enough, Hank. I won't take your bed."

She wouldn't budge on the sleeping arrangement so he brought her the quilt from his bed. While she burped Drew he doubled it and spread it on the floor between the bed and the drafting table to double as mattress and cover for the baby and then some.

When Drew finished, Mia glanced at the clock. "It's nearly midnight. You sure it's okay to call Mrs. Pearson this late?"

"She'll want to know so she can contact the family."

"That's a good point." Mia looked around. "Where's the phone?"

"In the kitchen. Give her my number as your contact. And give me the kid. I'll tuck him in."

"Thanks." She slipped over the end of the bed, now the only path to the kitchen.

While Hank changed Drew on the quilt, he eavesdropped shamelessly. Mia apologized for calling so late and then explained that she'd changed her mind about Drew. She loved him and wanted to adopt him herself. She was sorry for disappointing the other family, and would reimburse any plane fare. Yes, she assured the woman on the phone, she was certain about her decision and not about to change her mind.

After a silence, she sighed. "Oh. Of course. I've had a fire at my home tonight, and until the repairs are made I'm not sure where we'll be staying. Can I call you first thing Monday and let you know?" She thanked the woman and again apologized for any trouble.

She returned to the living room holding her pants up, looking exhausted but at peace—as peaceful as a woman who had just lost part of her home could look. "They're sending a social worker out next week," she said as she sat cross-legged next to Drew.

"What for?"

"To make sure I'll provide a good home for Drew."

"That sounds like a slam dunk," Hank said.

"You think?" Her mouth twisted in a wry smile. "Seeing as, at the moment I don't exactly *have* a home."

"But that's temporary. You'll show the social worker the cabin. That should satisfy him or her."

Her hands twisted at her waist. "I hope you're right."

Hank ached to pull her onto the bed and hold her. His fingers itched to slip inside the sweatshirt and slide up her smooth skin. He shoved his hands into his pockets. "If you need people to vouch for your mothering skills, tell them to talk to me. Or anybody from around here."

"I'll do that." For one brief moment she offered a joyous smile that lit her eyes. "Thank you, Hank, not only for what you did tonight, but for listening to my story about Gracie and helping me see the world differently. I owe you so much."

Damn, but she was pretty when she was happy. Basking in her warmth, he shrugged. "Hey, you did the work. I just pushed you in the right direction."

She planted a kiss on the baby's cheek. "Better turn out the lights. That'll make it easier for him to get to sleep."

Hank did, both in the living room and the hallway behind him. The light over the kitchen window remained on, bathing the room in soft shadows.

Mia rose from beside Drew. She sank wearily onto the edge of the mattress. "He'll be up again in a few hours. I'd better rest while I can."

"I hear that."

Hank was dead on his feet, yet his legs refused to carry him to the bedroom. He needed to be near Mia the way he needed air. At the same time, being near her was torture.

He wanted her so much. *Not gonna happen, buddy.* How many times did he have to remind himself? His jaw set.

As she pulled up the covers and settled into her pillow, she looked up at him. "What's on your mind, Hank?"

"I'm just glad you're alive."

"Yeah, me, too." She met his gaze across the dim room, her eyes big and dark.

He sensed that as tired as she was, she'd listen if he talked. He wanted to share his story almost as badly as he wanted to make love to her. He sucked in a breath, blew it out and opened his mouth. But his courage failed him.

The moment passed and she looked away. "Well, good night. Sleep tight."

"Back at ya."

He headed for the bathroom, knowing he wouldn't rest until he'd made things right with Mia. But he had no clue how to do that without getting hurt. He closed the bathroom door. She'd washed her bra and panties and hung them on the door hook to dry.

Sweet Christmas, underneath his sweats she was naked. His groin stirred as he turned on the shower. He stripped out of his sooty clothes and dropped them into the hamper. Standing in front of the three-quarter-length mirror on the wall, he checked out his body, trying to see it as Mia would. A dozen hideous scars, as puckered, red and jagged as if they were fresh, disfigured his belly, hip and lower back.

He recalled the horrified look on Kristin's face when she'd seen the damage. She hadn't even tried to hide her revulsion.

Mia was sure to feel the same.

Wincing, he turned from the mirror and stepped under the spray.

WHEN MIA HEARD the bathroom door shut she opened her eyes and kicked off the too big sweatpants that were falling down. Now that Hank was in the shower, she didn't have to be so modest or pretend to be asleep. So much had happened today, both horrible and incredibly wonderful, that her whirling mind refused to rest.

She'd lost possessions and a big part of the cabin, which was terrible. But she'd kept Drew safe. He was hers, or would be after the visit from the social worker. *I'm a mother.* Saying the words to herself felt wonderful. Smiling, she hugged her pillow. Hank had called her a great mom, but she knew there was plenty to learn. At least she now possessed the confidence to tackle the job, thanks in large part to Hank.

If that wasn't enough, he'd come to her rescue yet again, moving the animals to safety and helping her battle the fire. He was better than a guardian angel. Though she'd never be able to repay him, she'd gladly give him her heart—if only he'd take it. Unfortunately he seemed to want friendship but nothing more.

Regardless, she ached for him. Especially now. She longed to share his bed and feel the comforting warmth of his arms around her.

But not out of pity.

Not like what had happened after dinner tonight. The kisses and touches that had inflamed her had pushed Hank away. She let out a heavy sigh. Wishing things were different wouldn't change a thing. She'd learned that after Gracie died, and again after her parents left.

She *was* wrapped in Hank's big, warm sweatshirt. That was something, right? Hugging it close, she sniffed for his scent. The fabric smelled only of laundry detergent. Didn't that just figure.

Resigned and exhausted, she closed her eyes and slept.

HANK AWOKE at dawn to a doozy of a hard-on and the low murmur of Mia's voice as she crooned to Drew. He sat up and stretched, his sore muscles protesting from a week of hard work and battling last night's fire. Rest was what he needed. Instead he'd tossed and turned and tossed some more. How had he expected not to with Mia sleeping in the trailer?

After gritting his teeth for what seemed hours, he'd resorted to self-gratification. He gave a bitter smile. Hadn't helped much. His body craved sexual release with *Mia*. Not a chance of that.

Inviting her to stay here had been a bigger mistake than he'd originally thought. He'd do what he could to help her find another place. Today, if possible.

Despite his physical discomfort, despite knowing he could never make love with Mia, he was eager to see her and Drew. Which just went to show how dense he was. Frowning and cursing himself six ways to Sunday, he rose and quickly dressed.

And made up his mind. Today was a new day. From this moment on, he would not allow himself to want her.

As he entered the living room she was in the same sooty clothes she'd exchanged for his sweats last night and putting Drew on her shoulder. She'd transformed the Hide-A-Bed back into a sofa and piled the neatly folded quilt and sweats atop it. No longer pushed aside, the coffee table and armchair stood in their rightful spots.

As if she'd never slept here and didn't plan to again.

Hank's heart contracted, and he forgot that moments ago he'd decided she couldn't stay. "Leaving already?"

"Drew finished the last of the formula, and there's only one diaper left. I'm hoping a diaper or two survived the fire." Her expression darkened a moment and she hugged the baby closer. "I kept a jumbo box in his bedroom but of course, it's gone now.

"Dobson's carries that stuff," Hank said. *So don't run off just yet.*

"It doesn't open till eight." She glanced at the

clock on the wall. "One diaper won't last two hours. I've been known to stash a spare in the kitchen drawer with Drew's bath things. Cross your fingers."

Hank crossed fingers on both hands and held them up, gratified when he saw a smile. This morning her eyes were clear and her cheeks had color. She looked rested and healthy.

At least one of them had slept last night.

"I want to check on and feed the hawk, too," she said, moving toward the door. "This is his regular feeding time, and he'll expect his breakfast. Speaking of breakfast, I fed the dogs. I borrowed a can of tuna for Rags, too."

"What about you? Have you eaten?" Hank asked.

She shook her head. "For a man who works hard all day, you don't keep much food in the house." Her nose wrinkled. "How can a big guy like you survive on cereal?"

"It's the end of the week. I was planning a trip to the store today."

"Good to hear, but it doesn't help right now. I'd hoped to make breakfast for us."

The image of Mia puttering around his kitchen was as painful as it was pleasant. He enjoyed her cooking, but if she went to the trouble to cook for him, how could he ask her to leave?

He frowned. "Don't feel you have to make something." He peered into the cereal box. "There's enough here for both of us."

She grinned. "Thanks, but this morning I want more substantial food. After all the work you did last night, wouldn't you rather have sausages and pancakes?"

His mouth watered, and he couldn't turn her down. "I sure would."

Mia laughed, the sound lighting up the room. "My fridge is full of everything I need and more. If you think it's still safe to eat?"

It had been less than twelve hours since her power had gone out. "Refrigerators are heavily insulated. The food should be fine."

"Then Drew and I are off." She opened the door, letting in the fresh morning air.

"Are you sure you can handle going back there so soon?" Hank asked. By daylight the wreckage was sure to look worse than it had last night.

Mia gave a sober nod. "I know it won't be easy, but I want to see it before the insurance agent shows up later this morning."

She'd need emotional support. He followed her out. "I'll come with you and help you load up your car."

The early morning sky was cloud-free and rosy with dawn, but rain had fallen during the night and the cool air was free of smoke. They left the dogs fenced up. Rags accompanied them until a squirrel distracted him and he left to chase after it.

"I still haven't absorbed everything that happened yesterday," Mia said as they entered the stand of madronas.

"Hard to take in some of it," Hank said. "The fire, for one."

Hard, too, wanting Mia and not acting on his desire. Letting her think he didn't care for her because he feared what would happen if he expressed his feelings.

A drop of cold water dripped from a rain-soaked tree, hit his neck and slid down the back of his collar, a chilling reminder that he was right to keep quiet.

Oblivious to the torment plaguing him, she nodded. "I wouldn't wish a fire on my worst enemy. On the other hand, I'm a mother." A tender expression softened her face as she glanced down at her son. She smiled at Hank. "You're the first person to hear me say that out loud."

Overcome by her words and the emotion in her voice, Hank nodded. "I'm honored."

They walked in silence for a few moments. "How long do you think it'll take to rebuild the cabin?" Mia asked.

"A few weeks, maybe, or a month."

"That's not so bad." Their footsteps plodded over the packed earth under the trees. "I hope I can find an apartment with a thirty-day lease." She looked thoughtful. "Or maybe I'll house-sit, or take turns staying with different friends."

She'd broached the very topic Hank wanted to discuss. "With all the friends you have around here, you'll find something."

"I'm sure I will," she said without meeting his eyes.

He felt like a jerk but he didn't know what else to do. If she stayed under his roof again, he might do something he'd regret—get naked and climb into her bed. Darkness would hide his disfigurement until she touched his mangled skin. Then… Then he'd lose her. He pushed away the painful thought. He would not let that happen.

She had to leave.

Chapter Twelve

Mia stood outside at the back of the cabin, holding Drew and shivering in horror at what had been their bedrooms and bathroom. Chunks of blackened plaster from the walls and ceilings, charred support beams and broken glass littered the ground. The iron bedstead poked from a pile of rubble, and the chemical-stained mirror listed at an odd angle on what was left of the inside wall. These were the only items she recognized in the mess that was her bedroom.

She glanced at Hank and swallowed. "It looks a lot worse by the light of day."

"I know." Looking concerned, he started to reach for her but stopped himself, as if touching her was a bad idea. "You okay?"

She'd be better if he cared for her as deeply as she cared for him, but he'd made it clear that wasn't the case. As always, she was on her own. Drew shifted against her, reminding her that he was with her now, that they were a team. Filled with love and grateful beyond words, she hugged him close and felt her spirits lift.

Hank was staring at her, so she offered a fleeting smile. "I will be, after Martha Hicks takes another look around and files the insurance claim. At least then I can get this mess cleaned up."

"It's a good thing your friends volunteered to help, because there's a heck of a lot of work ahead." He looked around. "For now, you need a tarp over the back of the cabin to protect it from the elements. I'll see if I can get you one today."

Though Hank wasn't interested in her, he *was* a good friend. That was something to be thankful for. "Great."

"Ready to go inside?"

She nodded, then hesitated. "Do you think it's safe to bring Drew?"

"Probably, but if you're worried, do what you did last night. Strap him into his car seat. He'll be okay there."

He waited nearby while she secured Drew and tucked the bulky sweater around him. "I'm going to feed the hawk and get the groceries," she told her son. His little legs kicked, lifting her heart. "I love you, sweetie pie."

She turned toward Hank, catching him off guard.

He'd been watching her and Drew, his face full of naked longing and his eyes dark and so bleak, her heart ached.

Confused by his evident pain, and worried, she frowned. "Hank?"

In a blink he smoothed his expression to neutral, making her wonder whether she'd imagined his agony.

"Let's go," he said.

They walked into the kitchen together. Mia appreciated the company because suddenly her stomach twisted and her legs shook. Once inside she felt better. Other than the unpleasant smell of burned wood and smoke, the dirty boot prints the fire crew had left all over the linoleum and the fine layer of soot covering everything, the room looked as whole and solid as ever. That was comforting.

"Thank God the fire didn't reach this room," she breathed. "I don't know what I'd have done if I'd lost Gran's kitchen things. Especially her recipe box."

She pulled the old wood box from the shelf where she stored the cookbooks, then set it on the counter. "I'm bringing this with me." Opening the refrigerator, she peered inside. "It's still cold in here. I think the food's okay."

"Told you." Hank moved beside her and swung the door wide open. "Why don't you take care of the hawk, and I'll empty this thing."

Nodding, she took a packet of raw meat from the shelf. "There are grocery sacks under the sink."

After retrieving the protective leather glove from the clinic, which looked clean and smelled less like smoke than the living area, Mia stopped for a quick peek at Drew. He smiled at her, and suddenly her troubles seemed smaller.

"I'll be back soon," she said, returning the smile.

Humming softly, she headed for the flight cage. To her relief the hawk's screech was as deafening and hearty as ever. Despite the fire and his night outdoors, he looked healthy. She filled his water dish and quickly fed him.

When she returned to the kitchen, Hank was still at work. Hand on her hip, she shook her head. "What on earth is taking so long?"

He emerged from the depths of the refrigerator with both hands full and a crooked grin. "There's a lot of stuff in here. What'd you do, buy out Dobson's?"

"Compared to your empty refrigerator, anything would seem like a lot," she teased. "I'm hungry, so hurry it up."

"Slave driver," he mumbled as he went for another armful.

Bantering with Hank was fun, and working in the same room a pleasure. While Mia loaded two cans of formula into a sack and sought out diapers, she thought regretfully about leaving Hank and his trailer. She wished she and Drew could stay.

Then again, since she was in love with Hank and it wasn't mutual, living with him wasn't the best idea. She couldn't take the chance of making a fool of herself again by throwing herself at him. Besides, he hadn't invited her to stay.

She opened the drawer where she stowed Drew's bath things. "Look, a clean diaper," she announced, adding it to the sack. Two would be better, but she'd take what she got.

"Hallelujah." Hank peered from around the open refrigerator door and threw her a thumbs-up. "I'm just about through."

"Me, too." She tossed in a few of Drew's towels and the baby shampoo.

Making a quick stop in the utility room, she grabbed several cans of cat food and enough dog food to feed Ginger and pay Hank back. In companionable silence she and Hank loaded the car. By the time they drove down her driveway, Drew was yawning sleepily. She glanced at the clock on the dash. They'd spent less than an hour here, giving her plenty of time to make breakfast and eat before Dobson's opened.

The general store sold most everything a person could want, and Frank and Minnie Dobson were glad to order what they didn't carry. Mia planned to order a crib and other baby furniture, and to buy soy formula and diapers, baby blankets, undershirts and sleepers. For herself, new underwear, toiletries and a few outfits. Most important, a newspaper to search out another place to stay.

Hopefully by tonight.

HANK WASHED the breakfast dishes in his suddenly quiet kitchen. Mia had offered to help, but the thought of working beside her in the small space where they were sure to bump hips or elbows was torture. He'd made up an excuse about needing to work off the pancakes and wanting to tackle the mess by himself. Now she and Drew were on their way to Dobson's to shop, and then to meet the insurance agent at the cabin. They wouldn't be back for a while.

He had the trailer to himself, as he wanted. He'd always appreciated the peace and solitude, yet today the place felt lonely and way too quiet.

When Mia and Drew found somewhere to stay and moved out, it would be this way all the time. Instead of pleasing him, the thought put Hank in a rotten mood.

"Hell," he muttered at Ginger, Nugget and Rags, who'd come in for the leftover pancakes and sausage and were crowded together under the two-person café table.

"You think I should ask them to stay?" He pulled out the sink stopper and water gurgled rapidly down the drain.

Nugget and Ginger woofed. Rags yawned.

"Is that a yes?" Frowning, Hank rinsed and wrung out the sponge. "You guys don't know what you're talking about. That would cause nothing but trouble."

Abruptly both dogs scrambled up, barking as they raced for the door. Rags darted into the living room and ducked behind the sofa. Hank squinted out the kitchen window in time to see Jake's silver compact roll up the driveway. His brother and girlfriend had arrived.

No doubt the rest of the clan would soon follow. In the chaos of last night Hank had forgotten about the visit. He groaned. The timing wasn't the best, but at least Mia and Drew weren't here. That'd be hell to explain.

Wiping his hands on his jeans, he headed outside. He got to the car as Jake reached for the passenger's door.

With the canines dancing and yapping loudly, Hank grinned. "Look what the dogs dragged in."

His beaming brother paused to greet him. They stood nearly the same height and weight—Hank a bit taller and Jake stockier—and clapped each other on the back.

The rest of the family will be along soon," Jake

said over the noise. "Nugget looks good. Who's the other dog?"

"Belongs to my neighbor. Her name's Ginger."

The passenger's door opened and a tall, slender woman gracefully emerged. "Hey, doggies." She bent to rub each animal's head, making instant friends.

Jake turned toward her, his grin softening. "This is Jeannie. Jeannie, meet my kid brother, Hank."

He nodded at the attractive woman, who had to be close to six feet, almost as tall as him and Jake. He reached out a hand, but she shook her finger the way she probably did with the first graders she taught.

"None of that hand-shaking stuff for Jake's brother." She enveloped Hank in a quick, warm, vanilla-scented hug.

He must have looked as surprised as he felt, because both Jake and Jeannie laughed.

"See why I think she's special?" Jake said, kissing her nose. "She's so damn warm and sweet."

"Poor man is blinded by love." She showered him with an adoring look.

Envy punched Hank in the gut. Sure, he was happy for Jake. But he wanted what his brother had—with Mia. But that couldn't be.

"Speaking of love, we're only staying a few hours," Jake said. "I'm taking Jeannie to a romantic B and B on the coast for a couple of days."

She flushed and the couple shared a warm,

intimate look that had Hank wishing he were some-place else. "Sounds nice," he said.

When a minivan pulled up the driveway, Jake said, "That's Lisa and Ryan's new car. Mom and Dad came with them. They brought lunch, too."

"Good, because I didn't make it to the store." Suddenly uncomfortable and wary despite Jake's assurances, Hank watched the minivan roll to a stop.

Lisa, her red hair tied back, and her lanky husband, Ryan, exited, each with a bulging sack of food. Hank's plump, silver-haired mother and thin, balding father emerged from the back. A moment later the two kids scrambled out.

Genuinely glad to see them but on guard, he greeted his father and brother-in-law with stiff hand-shakes and his mother and Lisa with awkward hugs. The kids, seven-year-old Polly and five-year-old Tim, raced toward him, eyes bright and hair flying. Tim hugged his legs and Polly grabbed onto his waist. Together they nearly knocked him over with their joyous embraces. Hank laughed, and so did everybody else, breaking the ice.

Wanting in on the fun, Nugget and Ginger wagged their tails.

To Hank's relief, just as Jake had pointed out, as long as he didn't feel sorry for himself, no one seemed to pity him. He gestured toward the trailer. "It'll be a tight squeeze, but come on in."

Lisa brushed her coppery bangs from her forehead and frowned. "We'll come in after we see this house you're building."

Polly, whose hair was the same color, nodded. "Uncle Hank is going to win the 'tecture 'ward of the West."

"'Cause he's the best builder in the world," Tim added, eyeing Hank as if he were a superhero.

Accompanied by the dogs, Hank showed off the house and answered questions. The children soon grew tired of the talk and raced off to run and play— within sight of the adults.

"You're building a gorgeous home," his mother enthused a short while later. "That is, it will be when it's finished."

His father nodded and clapped an affectionate hand on his shoulder. "I'm real proud of you, son."

Hank puffed up with pride. "Thanks." It felt good to be with his family.

"I'd live here," Jeannie proclaimed, "only I probably couldn't afford it."

Everyone laughed.

"Plus it's out in the boonies," Lisa added.

"That, too. I'm a city girl."

"We're all city people," Ryan said.

"What about you?" Jake raised an eyebrow at Hank. "When are you coming back to Seattle?"

"As soon as I finish this project—another three-plus months on the house and two weeks after that, to finish the landscaping." Then he'd leave and never see Mia or Drew again. His chest felt empty, but he crossed his arms and shoved the thought from his mind. He nodded toward the trailer. "There's a scale model of the finished house inside. Take a look while I make coffee."

He penned up the dogs, then, opening the front door, gestured his family in. Wide-eyed, they piled into the living room. The kids made a beeline for the scale model, but the adults stopped inside the doorway.

"Whoa, look at the diapers and baby bottles." Jake slanted Hank a shrewd look. "Is there something you haven't told us?"

His mother's eyebrows rose high and his father pursed his lips. Jeannie, Ryan and Lisa shot him openly curious looks.

Bent on setting them straight, Hank quickly explained. "This stuff belongs to my neighbor, Mia. Part of her cabin burned down last night. She and her son stayed here."

Jake gave a knowing nod. "So that's why you hung up so fast. Are they okay?"

Hank didn't try to hide his relief. "Yes, thank God."

His mother, who seemed to have some sixth sense about his love life, caught his eye and nodded knowingly.

This time she was wrong.

Jake smirked. "You sly fox."

Lisa elbowed Hank. "You have a girlfriend and you never even told us."

Hank's mouth tightened. "She's not my girl-friend."

"Right," Ryan said. "And I'm not married to your sister."

Hank rolled his eyes. "You're so wrong."

The dogs' barking got Hank off the hook, until he saw that Mia's tan wagon had pulled up beside Jake's compact. The car door opened and she climbed out. She'd bought new clothes, Hank noted, jeans and a short-sleeve, purple blouse that showed her curves. She moved to the back door to unstrap Drew.

Tim and Polly raced to the window, followed by everybody else.

"That must be Mia," Lisa said as she peered out.

"She's cute," Jake observed. Jeannie arched her brow, and he quickly added, "Not as cute as you, honey. But a dam—er, darn close second."

She smiled at that before returning her attention to the window.

"I can't wait to meet her and her baby," Jake's mother said.

His dad nodded, his sister rubbed her hands together, and Ryan, Jake and Jeannie grinned.

"We're friends," Hank said, but the group was on its way out the door and wasn't listening.

He threw up his hands and followed them out. They'd figure things out soon enough.

"THE INSURANCE CHECK should be ready next week," Mia explained to the wonderful members of Hank's family as they relaxed in the living room of his trailer.

She'd been surrounded by them since they'd flocked to her car to meet her and Drew earlier. They'd asked dozens of questions about the fire damage and her clinic, so she'd led them through the trees and let them see for themselves. Later they'd shared their sandwiches, pop and cookies with her.

Now Mia sat on an armrest of Hank's sofa, beside Jeannie, a warm, open woman in her early thirties, who had begged to hold Drew and was feeding him. Hank's brother, Jake, flanked Jeannie's other side, arm slung around her shoulders. Their mother squeezed in beside Jake, and Lisa perched on the other armrest. Hank's father had the armchair. Ryan and Hank sat in chairs borrowed from the kitchen. Nearby, Hank's adorable niece and nephew sprawled on the floor, watching Drew with curiosity and interest. The small room was crowded but had never felt so warm and cozy.

Mia couldn't get over the family resemblance

between Hank, his siblings and parents. Brothers and sister all had their mother's whiskey-brown eyes. While Hank and Jake shared the same dark coloring as their mother, Lisa favored her fair-skinned, red-haired father.

Hank's father, a friendly man, cracked corny jokes, and his wife fondly indulged him with laughter. Lisa, too, laughed often, as did her husband. Jake smiled often, mostly at Jeannie. He was wild over her and not afraid to show it.

Only Hank seemed ill at ease. Stiff-shouldered and silent, he looked as if he'd rather be on a chain gang in Siberia than here. Mia wasn't certain why. She felt nothing but acceptance from these warm people, and envy that she didn't have a family like this.

"You gonna help Mia rebuild her place?" Jake asked Hank.

Before he could answer, Mia did. "He's busy enough with his own project. He works twelve-hour days," she told his family. "And he's already done so much for Drew and me. Driving us to the emergency room, helping stop the fire, putting us up last night. He's been amazing."

Hank's ears turned red and he waved away her words. "Anybody would have done those things. It's no trouble to help rebuild the cabin."

He didn't do well with praise. Maybe that was

why he seemed so uptight around the rest of the group, who complimented each other often.

Mia shook her head. "I won't take any more of your charity."

"Don't think of it as charity," Jake said. "Think of it as helping a neighbor in need. Nothing wrong with that." He shot his brother a knowing wink. "Right, Hank?"

"'Specially since she's pretty," his nephew, Tim, added.

Mia flushed, Lisa and Ryan exchanged looks with Mr. and Mrs. Adams, and Jeannie grinned. Hank scowled.

"I don't have anything else to do out here," he said as if that were his excuse for offering to help. "I'll work on your place nights and weekends."

Mia knew she'd never get over loving him if she saw him every day. And she definitely wanted to get over him. One-sided love hurt too much. "There are dozens of people around here looking for work. I don't need you, Hank."

The Adams clan stayed quiet, but they watched the conversation, their heads swiveling like spectators at a tennis match.

Hank's mouth tightened. "Look, I said I'd help."

"And I said—"

"Can't you two save the bickering till after we leave?" Jake said. He glanced at his watch. "Which will be soon, since Jeannie and I have quite a drive ahead."

Mortified, Mia snapped her mouth closed. Hank did the same.

"We ought to leave, too," Mrs. Adams said.

"Drew seems ready for a nap," Jeannie noted in a pleasant voice, glancing at the heavy-lidded baby in her arms. "Can I put him to bed before we go?"

"Sure," Mia said. Once Hank's family left, while Drew napped, she planned to comb through the apartment-for-rent section of the paper. Given the tension between her and Hank, the sooner, the better.

"Put him in the bedroom," Hank said. "Come on, I'll show you."

Tim and Polly jumped up. "Can we watch?"

"Why don't Grandpa and I take you outside?" Hank's mother suggested. "That way you can run off some of that energy before the drive back."

"Ryan and I need a stretch, too," Lisa said. Her husband nodded.

As soon as the front door closed and Hank and Jeannie disappeared down the hall, Jake aimed a friendly look at Mia. "I'm glad you came into Hank's life," he said in a voice too low for anyone but her to hear. "You've done him a world of good."

Mia corrected him. "You have that backward. Hank has helped me. If it hadn't been for him…" She wouldn't have Drew and the entire cabin might have burned down. Emotion clogged her throat. She swallowed and offered a tiny smile. "Let's just say, I owe him more than I can ever repay."

"It goes both ways. Last time I saw my brother, he was bitter. He didn't seem to care about much of anything. Now he's involved in the world, particularly the part where you are." Jake shot her a sober look. "That car accident and Gil's death…" He exhaled heavily. "And the thing with Kristin, happening so soon afterward…" He shook his head. "It's been a rough road."

Mia knew about the accident, but she'd never heard of the woman. She angled her head. "Who's Kristin?"

"Hank hasn't told you? Guess I put my foot in it," Jake said, no longer solemn, and far too cheerful to be contrite. "Better ask him about that. Personally, I'm glad they split up because I like you better." He grinned. "My brother's a lucky man."

Mia shook her head. "He doesn't have romantic feelings for me. We're just friends."

"Is that what you want?"

She stared at her hands, locked in her lap. "It's what Hank wants."

"Don't be so sure. I know my brother, and the way he looks at you…he's got it bad for you."

He certainly didn't act that way. Mia gave a wistful smile. "I wish that were true."

"Hank's a little gun-shy. Trust me, all he needs is a push in the right direction."

"You're saying I should throw myself at him?" Mia thought about how Hank had pulled away from her more than once when she wanted to make love, and her face heated.

"If that's not your style, you'll figure out something," Jake said. "Just don't give up on him. He needs you."

Jeannie's quiet laughter warned them that she and Hank were headed back.

"He's asleep," the woman said as she entered the room.

"Out cold," Hank seconded.

Mia smiled. "Good."

Jake stood. "It's a long drive to the coast. We'd best head out."

"Come back anytime," Hank said.

Jake and Jeannie collected their things. Outside, Hank penned the excited dogs. The brothers shared a quick embrace, and Mia and Jeannie did the same.

Jake hugged Mia. "Remember, don't give up on Hank," he whispered.

He winked. Then he and Jeannie climbed into their car. Hank's parents, sister and brother-in-law and kids piled into the minivan.

Mind whirling, standing in the afternoon sunshine beside the man she loved, Mia waved goodbye.

Was it possible Jake was right, that Hank liked her as more than a friend? That he *needed* her? *Give him a push,* Jake had suggested.

With Drew asleep, now was the perfect time to do just that. She had no sexy underwear and wasn't wearing makeup or fragrance. But she planned to seduce him—or die trying.

As Jake's car rolled down the dirt drive, she clasped Hank's firm biceps and leaned in close. "I have something for you."

"Oh?" Tensing, he scowled at her, but didn't pull away. "What?"

"It's a surprise." Wondering if she were a fool, but determined to follow Jake's advice, she wet her lips with the tip of her tongue. "Let's go inside."

Chapter Thirteen

"I like your family," Mia enthused as she and Hank entered the trailer. "You're lucky to have them."

With her pressed up close, one soft breast pushed against his arm and her eyes dark and full of promise, he could hardly think. "They can be nosy and pushy, but I guess they're okay," he returned.

"Mmm, you smell good."

She smiled up at him, her lips and eyes warm with meaning. She wanted him. Hank's body stirred but his mouth frowned. What in hell was she up to? They'd settled the physical thing, at least in his book. They weren't going there. Maybe she needed to hear it again.

"Look, Mia—" he warned as they walked into the living room.

"Shh. You'll ruin the surprise."

She pushed the door shut and turned the lock. Then, back against the white wood, hands behind her, she gestured with her chin toward the furniture.

"Sit down, Hank, and don't talk."

He'd never seen the bossy side of her. That floored him so much, he considered staying right where he was, a few feet into the room. But her determined expression compelled him to obey.

Shrugging, he headed for the armchair, where she couldn't sit beside him and drive him crazy with her soft body and lemon scent.

Cautiously he took his seat, crossing his arms over his chest. He stretched out his legs and waited for her to take her seat on the sofa. She didn't move from the door.

He eyed her suspiciously. "Don't you get to sit down?"

She shook her head. "That's part of the surprise." Holding the doorknob for support, she toed out of her ankle boots, removed her socks and stuffed them into her shoes.

Hank had never seen her bare feet. Like the rest of her they were small and slender. No polish on the toenails, and no toe rings. Plain, but sexy.

"Are you ready?" she asked in a seductive tone he'd never heard.

Every nerve in his body stood up. She shot an anxious glance at his face, so he nodded.

After sucking in a huge breath, then letting it out, she nodded. "Here goes."

Humming the tune of "The Stripper," she pulled

her shirt over her head, twirled it high and then tossed it aside. She was wearing the same white bra she'd hung on the bathroom door last night. Her breasts filled the cups. Hank couldn't see her nipples, but he remembered what they looked like— pink and proud. Suddenly the tips poked against the cotton as if he'd stroked her.

Wow. A certain part of his anatomy stirred. Shifting, he gripped the arms of the chair.

Her face was bright red now, and she wouldn't look directly at him. But she continued to hum. Hips wriggling, she eased her jeans down her slender legs and off. She stood in front of him in a pair of white cotton bikini panties. Licking her lips slowly with her tongue, she at last looked straight into Hank's eyes.

No doubt she saw the lust there. He swallowed. There was no way to hide his growing arousal, and he didn't try.

Gluing her gaze to his, Mia sashayed toward him, her progress seductive and painfully slow. Hank lost his patience and reached for her, tugging her to him. She straddled his hips, placed her palms on his chest, and leaned down to kiss him. The apex of her thighs pressed against his throbbing length, only the thin cotton of her panties and his jeans and boxers between them.

His already taut body roared to life. Her fingers

trailed lower and a groan ripped from his throat. He would take her here, now. If he left on his shirt…

No! He trapped her wrists, holding her—and himself—back. "What the hell are we doing?" he growled.

She gazed at him through half-lowered lids. "Let me do this, Hank. Let me show you how much I lo—like you."

The love and desire smoldering in her face burned through him to his very bones. The depth of her feelings awed and humbled him. He was unworthy of her, but God, how he hungered for her.

"I want you, too," he admitted in a hoarse voice, "so damn much."

A sensuous smile curled her lips. "Then make love with me."

Red-hot words, indeed. Need for her blotted out everything. In a desperate attempt at self-control he closed his eyes and blocked out her mesmerizing gaze. "Sweetheart, you don't really want me."

"I've never wanted a man more."

Her sure hands cupped and lifted his face, co-cooning him in warmth and subtly coaxing him to open his eyes. He did, and nearly lost himself in the deep, liquid blue pools that seemed to look into his very soul. Every nerve in his pulsing body urged him to take her, consequences be damned. The muscle in his hip spasmed painfully, reminding him of what would happen when she saw his body.

He tried to scoot back in the chair. That turned out to be a bad idea, for the movement rubbed the most honeyed part of her tighter against his swollen groin in sweet torture.

"Mia," he rasped through clenched teeth. "You're killing me." He didn't have the will to make her get off his lap. Hands on her hips, he shifted her off his sex.

"Who's Kristin?" she asked, catching him completely off guard.

He narrowed his eyes in suspicion. "What did Jake tell you?"

"Nothing, except to ask you about her. He said…" Pausing, she glanced at his strained fly. "That he knows you well, and that you like me a lot." When she again met his gaze, she wore a look of triumph. "If *you* don't, your body certainly does."

"It's not just my body."

"But?" she probed when he said no more. "Are you still in love with Kristin? Is that why you won't make love with me?" Hurt flashed on her face and her gaze shifted to his shoulder. "Or is there something about me you just don't like?"

He couldn't bear that he'd caused her to suffer. But was telling her the truth, showing her his mutilated body, worth his own pain? Because her reaction—disgust and repulsion—would hurt like hell.

He decided it was.

"I like everything about you," he said. "And no, I'm not still in love with Kristin. Looking back, I don't believe I ever was. It was more a sex thing between us. When that's all you have, it doesn't last."

Her eyes searched his face. "You broke up because the sex got old?"

He released a nervous, humorless, rusty-sounding laugh. "Not exactly."

Uncertain where to start or how to explain, and scared spitless, he blew out a breath and rubbed his hand over his face.

Mia clasped that same hand. "Just tell me, Hank."

Threading his fingers through hers, holding her gaze when he wanted to look away, he nodded. "You know about the night Gil died. But you don't know the details. He was driving my car. We'd been to a party and I'd drunk too much. He hadn't, so I handed him the keys. He took the freeway instead of the back roads I always used." Pausing a moment, he mustered the nerve to continue. "If I'd been at the wheel, that accident never would have happened."

"That doesn't mean it was your fault."

"I know that now," he agreed. "You helped me understand when we talked about Gracie. Gil's death wasn't my fault any more than Gracie's death was yours."

She nodded and smiled at him like an angel offering absolution. "What does that have to do with Kristin?"

Even with her warmth and encouragement, sharing the truth was difficult. The biggest risk of his life. A ragged breath tore from his chest.

"I got hurt in the accident. Badly hurt." Shoring up his courage, he swallowed. "Kristin couldn't handle what happened to my body."

"Your body? *What?*" Mia's voice rose, along with her eyebrows.

"I'm pretty scarred up."

Her jaw dropped. "If she broke up with you over a few scars, she must not have cared about you."

"I don't know, Mia. I'm really ugly." Refusing to flinch, he stated the raw truth. "Hideous."

"Show me." She scooted off his lap, but the warmth from her body lingered.

She offered him a hand. Taking it, he stood on legs rubbery with anxiety. He could change his mind and stop this whole thing now. But he needed and wanted to get it over with. Jaw set, he pulled off his shirt.

He caught his breath while Mia silently studied his mutilated belly. Face unreadable, she circled around his scarred side to his back. The waiting was agony. He clenched his hands into fists and wished to God he knew what she was thinking.

Suddenly he felt her fingers on the skin of his lower back, her touch soft and tentative. He tensed.

"Am I hurting you?" she asked in a voice that held not a trace of disgust.

He tried to speak. Cleared his throat. But nothing came out. So he shook his head.

She moved in front of him, her finger tracing a long scar from his back, around his side, to his stomach. "They aren't that bad."

"Don't mess with me," he warned. "I have eyes. I can see."

"So can I. What I see is an attractive man with a gorgeous body. Scars don't change that."

Her quiet statement stunned him. But he'd lived with the horror of his scars for so long, he was still wary. He eyed her, looking for signs that she might be lying—a grimace of disgust, a quick swallow of bile. "You're not repulsed?"

"No." She met his gaze straight on, her face shining and open, and shook her head. "Never."

Relief and an emotion so strong and fierce he couldn't identify it expanded in his chest.

She leaned down and kissed the puckered skin just beneath his navel. Blood roared through his body, hot and pulsing. Hands shaking, he pulled her up by the arms.

"Don't do that unless you mean it."

"I mean it." Her eyes were big and dark with desire. "I want you, Hank."

"There's more of the same on my hip." He was testing her, holding her with his gaze.

She didn't look away. "I'm more interested in what's between your hips." A teasing smile tugged her lips.

She reached for the button of his jeans.

"Wait." He held her at arm's length. "What about protection? It's been a long time for me. I don't have anything except for a two-year-old condom in my wallet. But I can pleasure you—"

"That wouldn't be fair," she interrupted.

"Touching you is all the satisfaction I need." He would enjoy watching her as she climaxed.

She stared blatantly at his arousal. "Somehow, I doubt that."

"This is no time for jokes," he admonished, but he also smiled. "We have a serious problem here. It's either satisfy you, or wait while I drive fifteen miles to the store and back."

"I can't wait that long," she said, "and it won't be good for me unless we share the pleasure. I haven't been with anyone in a long time, Hank. I'm clean."

"Same here."

"If we're both healthy, what's the problem?" She shot him a pleading look. "We don't need—"

"I don't want to get you pregnant."

"Good point," she said. "Let's go with a two-year-old condom."

Hank scooped his jeans off the floor and slid the wallet out of the pocket. He removed the foil packet from behind his driver's license and scrutinized it. "It's still sealed shut. I guess it's safe enough."

Her eyes shone, and he wanted her so badly, he thought he would burst. But there was one more detail to take care of.

"I want to do this right and make love to you in my bed," he said, "but with Drew in there, I'm afraid we're stuck out here, on the Hide-A-Bed."

They opened it together, silently tossing aside the cushions.

Hank dropped the foil packet onto the carpet beside the bed, then turned to her. "Now, where were we?"

"Mmm, here I believe." She fumbled with the button of his jeans in exquisite torture.

Hank groaned and tried to help.

"Let me do this by myself," she insisted. A moment later the button popped open. "Now the zipper." She worked it down over his strained sex.

Halfway down, growling, he circled her wrist and removed her hand. "Unless you want a quick and messy end to things, better let go."

She did. He stepped out of his jeans, kicked off his boxers and faced Mia.

The only woman he trusted.

MIA'S EYES fastened on Hank's groin. He was well-endowed and gloriously aroused. Because he wanted her. Heart thudding wildly, she unfastened her bra and shrugged out of it.

Hank dropped his heavy-lidded gaze to her breasts. His fingers trembled as he traced a line from the top of her breast to its peak. Sharp pleasure flooded her and her nipples beaded to hard points. He traced a path under her breasts, then returned to her nipples. She tipped back her head and thrust out her chest in a silent plea for more.

Growling his appreciation, he cupped her and gently squeezed. Moisture pooled between her thighs.

"Take off your panties," he said.

She peeled them off and stood in front of him. He took his time studying her, his smoldering expression making her feel sexy and desired.

"Beautiful," he murmured at last.

Mia smiled. "You're the beautiful one."

At her heartfelt words, his face filled with hunger and a tenderness that warmed her soul. She opened her arms.

Hank pulled her close. "You feel so good," he

said, and for a long moment, simply held her. Gently, as if he cherished her.

Mia released a soft sigh. If this wasn't heaven, it didn't exist. She tucked her head under his chin, certain she could feel his heart thundering—or was it hers?

She wanted to stay this close forever. Not that she expected forever with Hank. At the moment, she wanted only to make love with him. She nestled closer. The soft hairs on his chest rasped against her sensitive nipples. His swollen need prodded the apex of her thighs, and a throaty sound swelled between them. She dazedly realized it had come from her throat.

Tipping up her face, he captured her lips. The kiss was neither soft nor tender. His mouth was hungry and demanding, his hands fevered and eager on her skin.

Mia matched every caress with equal enthusiasm, losing herself in the sensation of Hank's mouth, his tongue, his hands, until her body felt as sultry and warm as heated honey. "I don't think I can stand any more," she gasped.

Hank's dark eyes glittered with heat. "Then lie down with me."

He pulled her onto the mattress. It dipped under their weight, the springs creaking. Pushing her onto her back, he leaned over her. Shooting her a wicked grin, he pinned her arms over her head. "Now I've got you right where I want you."

It was wonderful to see him smile. Mia started to smile right back, but he stopped her with a kiss. After thoroughly kissing her mouth, he moved to her earlobe. He nipped her neck, then her breast. His tongue circled the flesh, closer and closer to her aching nipple.

Craving his mouth, but unable to reach for him, she arched upward.

"Is this what you want?" He laved her nipple, then suckled.

A moan sighed from her throat.

"I take that as a yes." He showered the other breast with the same attention. Releasing her wrists at last, he kissed his way down her stomach, stopping at her navel.

Hot, moist air from his breath fanned her stomach and lower, teasing and frustrating. "Don't stop there," Mia pleaded, sounding impatient to her own ears.

"You kissed my belly," he said. "Now it's my turn."

He planted an openmouthed kiss below her navel. Need consumed her. "Please," she begged, twisting her hips.

Hank grinned again. "I like teasing you."

Despite the hunger burning her, she laughed and

struggled onto her elbows. "Oh, you devil. Let's see how you like it." She reached for his arousal, but he stopped her.

"I'm not through yet."

He kissed the insides of her thighs, where the skin was tender and sensitive. As his mouth moved nearer to the place that ached for his touch, she fell against the sheets, tense with anticipation. Dear heavens, how she loved and wanted him.

His hands slid up her legs. "Open for me, Mia."

He parted her most private parts and licked the sensitive nub. Sensation so intense it almost hurt rippled through her. She could have gone over the edge, but didn't want to go there without Hank.

She circled his shaft in her hand. "I want you inside me. Now."

"Sweetheart, that's exactly where I want to be," he said, his voice soft and hot. "Just hold on another minute."

He sheathed himself, then covered her with his body. Savoring the feel of his skin against hers, Mia closed her eyes. He entered swiftly, causing her to gasp with pleasure. She gripped his back, felt his taut muscles.

"I wanted to take it slow, but I…don't…think I can," he said through gritted teeth.

Her body coiled tight. "I don't want slow," she begged, lifting her hips.

She met him thrust for thrust, until he gripped her buttocks and his body jerked.

"Mia," he cried, plunging deep.

"I love you," she whispered, and her world exploded.

When she returned to the here and now, she lay sprawled over Hank's chest. His heart beat steadily under her ear and his arm curled protectively over the small of her back.

"That was amazing," he said, kissing her temple.

"It sure was. You are one great lover, Mr. Adams." Feeling his chest expand with pride, she smiled against his skin.

Making love with Hank had been perfect, so perfect, she'd told him she loved him.

Would her deep feelings scare him away?

He scooted out from under her as if in answer to her question. "Be right back." Buck-naked, he strode across the room without a trace of self-consciousness.

The scars were a small part of him. Mia was glad she'd helped him realize just how small, especially after he'd soothed her own internal scars. Tears of joy filled her eyes. Oh, how she loved him.

Too bad he didn't love her, too. He liked her, though, and he certainly enjoyed making love with her.

Was that enough?

She hugged the sheet to her body and sighed. It would have to be.

Chapter Fourteen

Standing in the bathroom, Hank pulled in a deep breath and squinted at the red, jagged scars crisscrossing his lower torso. Ugly, but not bad enough to push Mia away. She'd wanted him despite the scars, which amazed him.

Not only that, the sex had been fantastic. She was a willing, passionate partner. She'd said he was a great lover, and he knew she meant that. Feeling as if he'd just won the lottery, he grinned at himself like a fool.

She loved him. Her feelings for him filled him with wonder. And fear.

Mia was special. She needed a man worthy of returning her love and then some. Was he man enough to take on that responsibility? Could he take care of her and Drew the way they deserved? The daunting questions had him shaking in his boots.

Things were moving too fast. He needed time

alone to process both her feelings and his. Sober-faced, he turned from the mirror.

Knotting a towel around his waist, he returned to the living room. She was still in bed, the sheet pulled over her body, tucked under her arms, leaving her shoulders bare. Propped against the pillow, her light brown hair tangled from their wild sex, her eyelids heavy and her lips red and slightly swollen, she looked relaxed, thoroughly sated and desirable as hell.

Hank wanted to join her and make love to her all over again. Not a smart idea. They were out of condoms, and besides, there was too much to sort out.

"Think I'll pick up a few groceries," he said as he exchanged the towel for his shorts. "Better drive over to Dobson's now, before they close for the night."

"There's plenty of food in the refrigerator from my place," she reminded him.

True, but he needed to get out of here. "We need other stuff, too."

"You mean, a big box of condoms?" she teased.

Her open, loving expression made his heart swell, which unsettled him. He couldn't meet her gaze, couldn't return the smile. "Right, condoms."

"Hank…?"

"What?" He pulled on his jeans without meeting her eyes.

"Is something bothering you?"

Unable to share his thoughts, he shook his head. "Not really." *Coward.*

"I see."

He glanced her way. The hurt look on her face about killed him. He felt like a jerk—a totally confused jerk. He forced a tight smile. "You're imagining things, Mia. There's nothing bothering me, and there's nothing wrong." *Except that I'm scared out of my mind.*

She sat up, taking the sheet with her. Bit her lip. "Are you sorry we made love?"

"No," he stated, meaning it. "It was the best. *You* are the best…" At a loss for what more to say, he shrugged. He grabbed his socks and shoes and sat on the chair to put them on.

Her head angled a fraction. "But?"

"I'm not the right man for you."

"I see. And just how did you reach that conclusion?" Arms crossed over her chest, she looked like a woman determined to get answers.

He was too mixed up to give her what she wanted, and in no mood to try. Tight-lipped, he stood. "Can't this wait till I get back?"

His voice came out harsher than he'd intended, and she blinked and jerked as if he'd slapped her. "Mia," he said, "I didn't mean—"

"No need to explain, Hank," she said in an over-bright tone. "Last night Sookie invited us to stay with her. I think I'll take her up on the offer."

He didn't want her to go. He wanted her and Drew to stay here. Didn't he? He scratched the back of his neck. Right now he was too screwed up to know.

"Maybe that's a good idea," he said.

Avoiding his gaze, she nodded. "We'll be gone when you get back."

"If you need moral support when that social worker shows up, I'm here."

"And if you decide *you* want to talk instead of running away, *I'*ll be at the clinic on Monday."

Hank rolled his eyes. "I'm not running away."

"No? Well it sure looks that way to me."

In a foul mood, he opened the front door and headed out.

MIA WAITED for Hank's truck to roll down the driveway before rising. With an aching heart she gathered up her clothes and headed for the shower.

She turned on the water and stepped under the brisk spray, her eyes filling as she scrubbed away Hank's scent and the smell of their lovemaking.

Despite the fact that he'd rejected her, she wasn't sorry about loving him or telling him what was in her heart. She definitely wasn't sorry about making love with him. But she did have her pride.

The last thing she wanted was to burden him with her and Drew. They wouldn't stay here, and she'd never bother him again. Which was why she'd leave right away.

Clean now, she shut off the water. In a hurry to phone her friend, she quickly toweled off and dressed. Tiptoeing down the hall, she peeked at Drew, asleep on the floor in Hank's bedroom. Good. She had time to call Sookie and pack up their few belongings. If Drew awoke, she'd feed him in the car.

From Sookie's she'd look for a place to stay until the cabin was repaired. With a heavy heart Mia plodded toward the kitchen to call her friend.

USING THE HEM of his T-shirt, Hank wiped the sweat from his forehead and headed to the trailer for water. It wasn't quite 8:00 a.m., but the late May air was warm and he'd been hard at work laying cedar shingles on the roof, one square at a time, since first light. Already his back and arm muscles ached, but he didn't mind. The work was satisfying, and ensuring the alignment of each square and then hammering it into place kept him too occupied to think about Mia.

It had been four days since he'd seen her, but it felt like forever. He missed her, yet the thought of settling down with her and Drew continued to scare the hell out of him. His brain felt all snarled up and his mood was as rotten as it had been Saturday when he'd left the trailer after their fight. He could hardly stand his own company.

Even Nugget avoided him. The dog kept to his doghouse, from time to time eyeing Hank mournfully. The mutt probably missed Ginger and Mia and Drew.

Coming out of the trailer, Hank saw John, Pete, Lester, Tommy and Del drive up, their assorted cars and trucks forming a line. The whole crew, except for Bart Patterson.

Hank greeted them with a frown. "Where's Patterson?"

"Good morning to you, too." Hitching his jeans over his belly, John shrugged. "He'll be here."

On cue, the missing crew member's old maroon car pulled into the drive. "What'd I tell you?" John gestured toward the vehicle. "There he is."

The men headed for the house to start work. Hank waited for Bart to park and exit. As the man ambled toward him, he glanced at his watch and scowled. "You're late."

"Only by five minutes." Bart looked surprised. "You're in a hell of a mood this morning."

Hank kicked a pebble across the grass. "What if I am?"

His employee held up his hands in a gesture of surrender, and they followed the others to the house.

"Want to know why I'm late?" Bart said. He didn't wait for Hank's reply. "Because Mia had a meltdown."

Hank knew she'd been staying with Bart and Sookie. He frowned, his bad mood replaced by concern. "What's wrong? Is she sick? Is Drew okay?"

"It's nothing like that," Bart said. "It's this social worker business. Some lady named Mrs. Plotter set up an appointment for ten-thirty this morning. Mia's afraid she won't like her or the cabin. She thinks Mrs. Plotter will take Drew away from her."

Hank's protective hackles rose. Eyes narrowed, he strode toward the ladder leading to the roof. "I said I'd vouch for her if she needed me," he stormed as he climbed the rungs. "Why didn't she ask me?"

"Hey," Bart said from behind him, "don't take this out on me. It's not my fault you two aren't getting along."

Hank rolled his eyes. Everybody seemed to know that after spending one night together, he and Mia had parted ways.

If you decide you want to talk, I'll be at the clinic, she'd said. So far, he'd stayed away, mainly because, though he knew what she needed, he wasn't so sure about himself.

She hadn't exactly tried to contact him, either, even about the social worker. Maybe she *didn't* need him anymore. Seriously peeved, jaw set, he edged onto the roof with the rest of the crew. He picked up his hammer and pounded a cedar shingle with unusual force.

Lester, the only one who didn't seem cowed by Hank's menacing mood, shook his head. "Maybe you ought to get over there before that social worker shows up."

"I wish he would," Bart muttered.

All six men exchanged wary looks, then bent intently to their work.

What the hell? "If you have something to say, spit it out," Hank snarled. John was the oldest and often spoke for the others. Hank jerked his chin at the burly man. "John?"

At first the older man looked taken aback. Then he shrugged. "Since you asked, I'll give it to you straight. You've been a pain in the butt for days now, Hank. We all know it's because you're in love with Mia and something went wrong between you. Why don't you put yourself out of your misery and patch things up with her?"

Hank rubbed his hand over his chin. Did he love Mia? Could something like that be clear to everyone else yet invisible to him? The answer came without hesitation. *Yes.* He loved her. Admitting it to himself felt good.

"Maybe I will," he said.

"If I were you, I'd get over there right now," John advised. "That way you'll have plenty of time to make up before you help her with that social worker business."

Suddenly Hank couldn't wait to do just that. But he hesitated. After the shabby way he'd treated her, he wasn't sure she'd listen.

"What would you say if you were in my shoes?" he asked his crew.

Del and Tommy pointed at Pete. "He's the expert on women."

Pete shrugged. "I'd tell her all that mushy stuff women like to hear. That you love her, and she's pretty, and whatever else you can think of."

Deep in thought, Hank nodded. It was time to tell Mia he loved her. He only hoped it wasn't too late. "Think I'll clean up and take a walk," he said.

Nugget yipped from the dog run and all six crew members threw him a thumbs-up.

SITTING on a hard, orange chair in an empty exam room, Mia cuddled Drew, who refused to take his nap. Thanks to cleaning supplies and zealous friends, the clinic was in good shape. But she wasn't ready to reopen just yet. She was too nervous about the visit from the social worker, a no-nonsense woman named Mrs. Plotter. That was her only reason for being here today, to show the social worker the cabin and clinic.

Drew sensed her tension and had fussed unhappily all morning. She couldn't seem to comfort him. No doubt Mrs. Plotter would find her parenting skills sorely lacking.

What if she decided Mia wasn't good enough to be his mother?

Sookie, who'd come with her for moral support, poked her head in. "I hope you don't mind that I just scheduled two appointments for the end of next week," she said.

By then the whole social worker thing would be behind her, and hopefully the adoption process well on its way. Mia nodded. "That sounds about right."

Drew began to cry. With a weary sigh, she tried to comfort him. In vain. Stiffening, he screamed.

"Hush," she said, knowing the baby wouldn't understand.

Naturally he howled even louder. She bit her lip. If only Hank were here… But he wasn't, and she refused to rely on him ever again. Her broken heart ached, but that was the way it was. The crying baby kicked and shook his fists, as if the situation incensed him.

"Let me take him for a while," Sookie offered over the noise.

Though Mia badly needed a break, she shook her head. "Better not today."

Her friend peered at her with concern. "You okay?"

She shook her head. "I'm scared. I don't want to lose Drew."

"I know, hon." Her friend patted her shoulder and shot her a sympathetic smile. "It'll all work out."

Mia wasn't so sure.

The front doorbell buzzed. Everybody knew the clinic was closed. Her stomach clenched. "What if that's the social worker, and she hears Drew screaming?"

"Two hours early?" Mia's friend shook her head. "I doubt that's her. You stay here with your son. I'll send whoever it is away."

Drew sucked in a breath, quiet for a moment, and Mia heard voices. Then he started up again and she heard nothing but him.

The door opened. Grinning like a woman with a delicious secret, Sookie returned. "You have a visitor, and it isn't the social worker." Before Mia could ask who, her friend snatched Drew. "I'll take him and try to get him to sleep. Go on in," she said as she left with the baby.

Hank moved into the room, hands in his pockets, as handsome as ever.

What was he doing here? She managed a cordial but cool nod. "Hello, Hank."

"How are you?" he asked.

"I've been better." She tried to smile, but her nerves wouldn't allow it. "Do you want to sit down? I can get another chair from the exam room next door, or…"

"I'd rather stand." Shifting uncomfortably, he cleared his throat. "I came to, uh, talk."

Was that good or bad? Anxious, nervous and dying of curiosity, she managed to contain herself. "Okay."

"What you said about me running away. You were right. Thing is, I was scared." He glanced at the floor and cleared his throat again. "I've never been in love before and—"

"What was that?" Certain she'd heard wrong, Mia cupped her ear and frowned.

"I love you," he said, staring straight into her eyes.

Speechless, she closed her gaping mouth and sank against the chair. "Oh."

Hank's face fell. "I guess you changed your mind about me."

"No." She gave her head a rapid shake. "I still love you, Hank. It's just, you caught me by complete surprise."

"I was too dense to figure out my own feelings but I know better now." Taking her hands, he pulled her to her feet. "Are you too mad to forgive me for screwing up?"

Hank loved her. A warm, cozy feeling crept through her. "Silly man." Smiling, she caressed his cheek. "I'm not mad at you."

He let out a breath and wrapped his arms around

her. "Thank God. I've missed you," he said. His lips claimed hers and she was home.

A long while later, after her bones had melted and the world had faded to Hank and only Hank, he pulled back without releasing her.

"I heard about the social worker."

She nodded, hugging him. "I'm scared. What if she takes Drew from me?"

He kissed her temple. "Like I said the other day, you're a fine mother. I'll tell her so. I sure wouldn't want anybody else to mother my kids." He swallowed. "That is, if you'll marry me and let me adopt Drew." His hopeful gaze searched her face. "What do you think?"

"Yes, Hank, I'll marry you and let you adopt Drew. Only…"

Worry lines etched his brow. "What?"

"I've never lived in a big city before. I'm not sure how well I'll adjust."

"Big city?" He laughed. "You're not moving anyplace. I'll relocate my company here. We'll move into the house I'm building and I'll use the non-clinic part of the cabin as my office." Pausing, he searched her face. "Unless you'd rather live in the cabin. Then I'll rent space in town. Anything you want, just as long as I'm part of the package."

His words filled her with sweet warmth. "Oh,

Hank, you are. And I'd love to live in that beautiful house. But what about the award?"

"Moving into the house won't affect the judging." He tipped up her chin. "Do you mean it? You'll marry me and live in that house?"

Smiling broadly, she nodded. She started to pull away. "I can't wait to tell Sookie—"

"Not just yet." Hank nibbled her earlobe, sending thrills through her. "I want you to myself a little longer." He glanced at the wall clock. "We have more than an hour before the social worker arrives." With a sly grin he slid a condom from his pocket. "Is there a way to lock that door?"

Feeling wicked and loved, Mia giggled as she flipped the latch.

LOCKING MIA'S HAND in his, Hank watched Dorothea Plotter, the somber, fortysomething social worker prop her worn brown briefcase on the hood of her sedan.

"Thanks for showing me around the cabin and the beautiful new home you're building," she said.

Mia had strapped Drew to her chest. Her free hand hovered nervously near his head. Hank gave her a reassuring smile and nodded toward the social worker. *Ask her about Drew.* She shook her head.

Too scared to ask, he figured. So he did it for her. "What's the verdict? Do we get to keep Drew?"

Mrs. Plotter shaded her eyes with her hand and

looked from Hank to Mia to the baby. "It's obvious to me that Mia is a good mother and you're a doting father. Fine parents indeed," she said. "In my opinion, Drew is a very fortunate child." She smiled at Mia. "He's yours. I'll draw up the paperwork this afternoon."

Sagging in relief against Hank, Mia beamed, her joy brightening the already sunny morning. "Thank you, thank you so much."

Her smile was so beautiful, so contagious, that Hank grinned, as well. "That's great news. Congratulations, Mom," he told Mia.

Her smile broadened and her eyes filled. "This is the best day of my life," she said, and Hank felt as if he were the luckiest man alive.

"Would you like to come to our wedding?" he asked the social worker. Mia shot him an approving nod.

"I believe I would," Mrs. Plotter said. "When exactly is it?"

Eyes shining with love, Mia gazed up at him. "When is it, Hank?"

He couldn't wait to make her his wife. "As soon as possible," he said.

Epilogue

Four months later

"Nervous?" Hank asked as he studied his wife.

"A little." Twisting her hands, Mia scrutinized the polished mahogany table in their brand-new dining room, her gaze on the vase of early fall wildflowers he had picked. "This is the first meal I've cooked for your family."

"It'll be great," he said, pulling her close.

Drew bounced happily in his indoor swing, a gift from Jake and Jeannie, and giggled. Mia shot the boy a quick smile that faded as she glanced anxiously at Hank.

"Do you think they'll like beef stew and biscuits?"

"No doubt in my mind." He grinned. "After all, when you cooked it for me you won my heart. Your stew and those burned biscuits are the reason I married you."

Mia laughed, the sound like the soft, summer breeze. "Did you hear that, Drew? Your daddy married me under false pretenses."

She stood on her toes and kissed Hank's chin. Fire roared in his blood and his body responded with amazing speed. Lowering his head, he captured her lips. Drew made a gurgling sound, and they broke apart, gasping and laughing.

"Happy?" Hank asked.

Mia showered him with a radiant smile that warmed the whole room. She glanced around at the beautiful house that had won the Architectural Award of the West, the place they now called home. "I'm in love with a man who loves me. We have a son and a wonderful extended family. My best friend is pregnant. Yes, I'm totally and completely happy."

Through the window, a hawk—the same raptor she'd rehabilitated and set free—shrieked and swooped low before soaring into the sky. Drew crowed and pointed at the bird.

"That's the red-tailed hawk," Mia told him.

Suddenly the smoke detector squealed.

"My biscuits!" She rushed into the kitchen.

Drew let out a howl matched by Ginger's sharp yips and Nugget's mournful cry. Rags darted across the dark oak floor and disappeared down the hall.

The doorbell rang, announcing Hank's family. He grinned. Life didn't get any better than this.

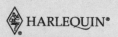

HARLEQUIN®

American **R O M A N C E**®

IS DELIGHTED TO BRING YOU FOUR NEW
BOOKS IN A MINISERIES BY POPULAR AUTHOR

Mary Anne Wilson

RETURN TO *Silver Creek*

In this small town in the high mountain country of
Nevada, four lucky bachelors find love where they
least expect it. And learn you can go home again.

JACK AND JILLIAN
(#1105)
On sale March 2006

Also look for:

DISCOVERING DUNCAN (#1061)
JUDGING JOSHUA (#1078)
HOLIDAY HOMECOMING (#1092)

Available wherever Harlequin books are sold.

www.eHarlequin.com

HARSCMAR

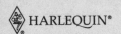

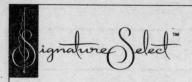
Signature Select™

A good start to a new day…or a new life!

National bestselling author

ROZ
Denny
FOX

Coffee in the Morning

A heartwarming volume of two classic stories
with the miniseries characters you love! A
wagon train journey along the Santa Fe Trail
is a catalyst for romance as Emily Benton and
Sherry Campbell each find love.

On sale March.

The story continues in April 2006 with
Roz Denny Fox's brand-new story,
Hot Chocolate on a Cold Day.